"Animals shouldn't *be* like this!"

The minute they walked inside, Val cringed. It smelled terrible. There were cages ranged around the tent in which sleepy-looking animals lay, their eyes half closed.

"Dad, I don't like this," Val whispered, taking her father's hand. "Animals shouldn't *be* like this!"

"You're right, Vallie," Doc said. "We'll leave right away."

"Hey, Vallie, come look at this monkey!" Teddy was peering through the bars at a small capuchin monkey. A sign over its cage said "Gigi." Gigi was huddled in a corner of its cage. Its eyes were bleary and filled with mucus. As Val looked at it, it looked back at her, and there was something in its beseeching gaze that wrung her heart.

ANIMAL INN

MONKEY BUSINESS

Virginia Vail

SCHOLASTIC INC.
New York Toronto London Auckland Sydney

ISBN 0-590-40183-1

12 11 10 9 8 7 6 5 4 3 2 1 7 8 9/8 0 1 2/9

Printed in the U.S.A. 11

First Scholastic printing, February 1987

Chapter 1

"Hey, Val! Erin! Dad! Guess what!"

Teddy Taylor dashed through the front door of the Taylors' big stone house on Old Mill Road, followed by his two best friends, Eric and Billy. They dropped their football helmets on the floor with a clatter. Jocko, the shaggy little black-and-white mongrel, and Sunshine, the big golden retriever, welcomed the boys with happy barks. Teddy grabbed Jocko around the middle and lifted him up in the air, swinging him around in a circle.

"Hey, cut that out!" Eric giggled as Sunshine licked his face with a wet pink tongue.

Val and her best friend, Jill Dearborne, had been sitting at the dining room table playing a game of Clue. Now they came into the living room to see what all the fuss was about. Jill clapped her hands over her ears.

"Quiet down, you guys!" she cried. "You're giving me an earache."

"Yes, Teddy, cool it," Val added. "And don't

throw Jocko around like that — if you dropped him, he might get hurt. Hi, Eric, Billy. Guess the Tigers won the game, right?"

"Nope," Billy said. "The Buffaloes creamed us, twenty-four to six. They're not called 'the thundering herd' for nothing."

"So why all the shouting?" Val asked.

" 'Cause a carnival's coming to town!" Teddy told her. "We saw the posters. They're all over the place! It's gonna be at the fairgrounds next week — lots of rides, and games, and a special zoo called a 'nagery!"

"A what?" Jill asked.

"A 'nagery — you know, like lots of wild animals?"

"You mean a *menagerie*," Val corrected.

"That's what I said, dummy!" Teddy scowled at his big sister. "What's the matter with you two? Something wrong with your ears?"

Val and Jill looked at each other and grinned.

"I told you you were giving me an earache. Guess I'm going deaf," Jill teased.

"What's happening? What's all the noise about?"

Val and Teddy's eleven-year-old sister, Erin, came into the room. She had been practicing ballet in the basement, and was wearing her leotard and tights.

"A carnival's coming to town, Erin," Teddy said. "And we're all gonna go, right, guys?"

Eric and Billy nodded.

"Oh, great!" Erin said happily. "I love carnivals. Does Daddy know? Let's ask him to take us all!"

"Where *is* Dad?" Teddy asked Val.

"He's up in his study, watching a football game on TV," she said. "I bet he'll be glad to take us to the carnival. Remember last year when he hit the target and knocked the clown into the water on the very first throw? He won an alarm clock."

"Yes, and then we all went on the Spider Sky-ride, and Erin got sick and threw up all over the place," Teddy put in cheerfully.

"Thanks for reminding me," said Erin, making a face. "If this carnival has a Spider Skyride, count me out. But I love the merry-go-round and the Ferris wheel."

"Hey, Val, is there anything to drink?" Teddy asked. "Me and Billy and Eric are so thirsty we're gonna die if we don't have some lemonade or some-thing."

"I'm kind of thirsty myself," Val admitted. "C'mon, Jill. I know there's some frozen lemonade. We'll make a pitcher, and there are some of Mrs. Racer's fudge nut brownies left over from last night."

"I'll help," Erin said. "You're such a terrible cook, Vallie, you'll probably manage to *burn* the lemonade!"

Val gave her sister a dirty look. "I can't burn it if I don't cook it, can I?"

"*You* could!" said Erin.

As the three girls headed for the kitchen, Val heard Teddy say, "C'mon, guys, let's turn on the TV. The Eagles are playing the Rams. Hope the Eagles do better than the Tigers did today."

"Maybe Mrs. Racer will want to come to the carnival, too," Erin said, opening the freezer compartment of the refrigerator and taking out a can of frozen lemonade.

"Maybe. We'll ask her when she comes in on Tuesday," said Val.

Mrs. Racer was the Taylors' housekeeper who had taken care of the family ever since Mrs. Taylor had died in an automobile accident three years ago. Her days off were Sunday and Monday, which were the days on which Dr. Theodore Taylor's Animal Inn was closed. Today was a Sunday, so Mrs. Racer was not there.

Cleveland, Val's big, fat orange cat, jumped up on the kitchen counter as Val dumped the can of frozen lemonade into a pitcher. Cleveland was purring his head off, rubbing against Val and keeping his big yellow eyes on the pitcher.

"No, Cleveland, this is *not* milk," Val told him sternly. "And you know you're not supposed to be up here, anyway." She turned to Erin. "Erin, put some milk in Cleveland's bowl before he attacks the lemonade."

Jill picked up the cat and set him down next to his special bowl. It was one Val had made in ceramics class, and it had his name on it in bright blue letters.

"Cleveland, you are one spoiled cat," Jill said, stroking his thick fur. Cleveland just narrowed his eyes at her (Val called it "squinging") and waited patiently while Erin poured fresh milk into his bowl.

"Let's ask Daddy to take us to the carnival next Monday after school," Erin said. "You come, too, Jill, okay?"

"Okay!" said Jill. "That'd be great."

"If Mrs. Racer wants to come, we can pick her up on the way," Val suggested. "It'll be lots of fun. I can almost taste the cotton candy and the candy apples now. And maybe this year I'll win a prize at one of those stands where you throw balls at stuffed cats."

Cleveland looked over his shoulder at her, almost as if he understood what she had said and didn't like what he had heard.

"Not *real* cats, Cleveland," Val told him hastily. "Just funny-looking toys."

Cleveland switched his tail and went back to his bowl of milk.

"You have to be pretty good to knock those

things down," Jill said. "My dad told me they're so heavily weighted at the bottom, and the balls are so light, that you have to be a real expert to win anything."

"My pitching's getting better," Val said. She was on the Hamilton Junior High girls' softball team and had been working on strengthening her pitching arm. "I bet I'll win something this year."

"Lemonade's ready," Erin sang out. "The brownies are in that metal box next to the flour canister, Jill. But if we want to eat any of them ourselves we'd better do it now, because once Teddy and his pals get hold of them, forget it."

"Lemonade? Brownies? Lemme at 'em!" Teddy shouted as he, Eric, and Billy burst into the kitchen.

Jill stared as the boys snatched handfuls of brownies and glasses of ice-cold lemonade. "How could they hear Erin over the sound of the TV all the way in the living room?"

Val gave her little brother a wry look. "Teddy can hear a brownie a mile away. The way he eats, he ought to be as fat as a pig, but he's not."

"I'm a growing boy and I need lots of good, nourishing food," Teddy announced with an angelic smile. "C'mon, guys, the Eagles are winning. Bring your stuff into the living room."

"Don't you dare get crumbs all over the carpet," Erin called after him as the boys charged out of the kitchen. "Mrs. Racer just vacuumed yesterday."

"No problem," Teddy said cheerfully. "If we drop any crumbs, the dogs'll eat 'em before they hit the floor."

Val sighed. "He's probably right. Any brownies left in that tin, Jill?"

"Three and a half, but the half is kind of hard and dry," Jill said.

"Plenty of lemonade, though," said Erin. She poured lemonade into three glasses and she, Val, and Jill took the rest of the brownies and their drinks to the butcher block table.

"All *right!* Touchdown!" Teddy hollered, and Eric and Billy whooped with joy.

Val reached out and closed the kitchen door. "Peace and quiet at last," she said, grinning at Erin and Jill.

"I kind of like it — all the action around here, I mean," Jill said, taking a bite out of her brownie. "My house is always so quiet. It's nice sometimes, being an only child, but I wouldn't mind having some brothers and sisters."

"I'd *love* being an only child," Erin said fervently. "Well, not all the time, just sometimes," she added as Val scowled at her. "I mean, it would be nice to be able to get the *good* brownies once in a while instead of leftovers."

"Want to trade?" Jill asked, laughing.

Erin laughed, too. "No, I guess not. Little brothers are a pain — and big sisters can be, too" — she made a face at Val — "but I love my family, so I'm pretty satisfied the way things are."

"That's good," Val said. "Because *you* can be a pain, too, but most of the time you're okay. And one day, you're going to be a famous ballerina and we'll all be proud of you."

A dreamy expression passed over Erin's face. "Yes, I will be. I just know it! Mommy was a real ballerina when she was young. . . ."

"And I'm going to be a vet, like Dad," Val said. She turned to Jill. "What are you going to be when you grow up, Jill? This week, I mean?"

It was a standing joke between Val and Jill that Jill's plans for her future changed every other day.

"I am definitely going to be an interior decorator," Jill told her firmly. "Like my mom. Unless I decide to go to law school and become a lawyer like Dad. Or maybe I'll be a fashion designer. Or maybe — "

"In the meantime," Val interrupted, "you're going to the carnival with us next week, right? It'll be lots of fun. I love carnivals — only I really kind of hate those menageries. I don't like to see animals cooped up in cages. That's why I don't like zoos, either. Animals shouldn't be confined, away from their natural habitat. It's not right."

"Oh, Vallie," Erin sighed. "How else would people get to know what wild animals really look like? And I bet they're perfectly happy, being fed regularly and being taken care of. If I were a tiger, I'd like to know that I didn't have to go out and hunt for my dinner — it would be delivered to me whenever I wanted it."

Val shook her head. "No, you wouldn't. You *think* you'd like it because you're not a tiger, you're a person. But a tiger — or a lion, or any big, beautiful wild animal — needs to follow its natural instincts, or else it gets sluggish and turns into a pet. And if it turns into a pet, it's not a wild animal anymore. Remember the movie *Born Free*? That's why the Adamsons worked so hard to teach Elsa, the lioness, how to behave like a real lion, not just an overgrown pussycat."

Rrroowww!

"Speaking of overgrown pussycats, I think Cleveland has had it with being ignored," Erin said.

Cleveland leaped up into Val's lap and rubbed his big orange head against her chin, purring loudly.

"Okay, Cleveland. There's one little crumb of brownie left," Val said. The cat sniffed at the morsel she held between her fingers, then delicately took it, munching happily.

"That is one cat who would never, *ever* be happy without at least four meals a day, delivered right into his bowl," said Jill. "Not to mention snacks."

"But Cleveland's a house cat," Val reminded her. "If he were a lion or a tiger, he ought to be out there on the African plains, chasing after antelopes and stuff like that."

"But wouldn't you feel sorry for the antelopes?" Erin asked. "You're so crazy about animals — how can you say that lions and tigers ought to eat *other* animals?"

Val thought about that one for a while. Finally she said, "It's different. You can't expect an animal to go against its nature and start eating salad when it's natural for it to eat meat. I'm a vegetarian because I don't *like* to eat meat. That's my choice. But animals don't have a choice. Cows eat grass, and horses eat oats, and Cleveland. . . ."

"Cleveland eats *everything*," Jill said, giggling. "I bet even if I gave him stinky old Limburger cheese, he'd eat it."

"You're right," Val said. "Cleveland loves cheese — and cooked corn and asparagus and chicken and just about anything that ends up on his plate."

"Like Teddy," Erin put in, and they all laughed.

"Any more brownies?" Teddy poked his head into the kitchen, looking hopeful.

"Not a single crumb," Val told him. "You're out of luck."

"Rats!" Teddy frowned. "Oh, well. When's supper, Vallie? And can Billy and Eric eat over?"

"Supper's in about an hour and a half," Val said. "And I guess they can have supper with us, but they have to call their mothers and get permission."

Teddy's head disappeared, and Val asked Jill, "Want to eat over, too? I'm going to put a chicken in the oven to roast." She added hastily, seeing Jill's concerned expression, "It's okay. Mrs. Racer showed Erin how to stuff it. It won't be like the last time, when I stuck the chicken in the oven with all the giblets still in the plastic bag inside it. This one has *real* stuffing. And I'm going to have eggplant Parmesan."

"Well, maybe," Jill said. "I'll have to call my mom. You're *sure* we won't be eating plastic?"

"Cross my heart and hope to die," Val told her. "And if you don't like it, there's lots of eggplant."

"Yuck!" Jill finished off the last of her lemonade and set her glass down on the table. "Chicken sounds good. Eggplant sounds disgusting. But I'd like to stay, and then we can go over our English homework for tomorrow. And I'll ask Mom if I can go with you to the carnival. I'm sure she'll say yes."

"Why don't you ask Toby to come to the carnival, too?" Erin suggested. "Living way out on the Currans' farm, I bet he doesn't even know about it."

"Good idea," Val said. "I'll ask him Tuesday when we're both helping Dad at Animal Inn after school."

Toby Curran was Val's other best friend. The Taylors had practically adopted him into the family since he'd started helping Doc and Val at the clinic. He was like a big brother to Val, Erin, and Teddy, and though he and Val didn't always see eye to eye, most of the time they had fun together.

Jill picked up the kitchen phone to call home, put it to her ear, then sighed and hung up. "Eric beat me to it. He's calling *his* mom. Gee, Val, are you sure there'll be enough food to go around? What with Eric and Billy and me, that makes seven people."

"No problem," Val told her. "This is one big chicken! It came from Mr. Gebhart. Ever since Dad tried to save little Amos Gebhart's collie after it was hit by a car, Mr. Gebhart and Amos come by every week with chickens, or eggs, or produce from their farm."

"Yes," Erin put in, "and they gave us the chicks who live in the coop out back. It's neat, because they drive up in their Amish buggy. Vallie's become great pals with their horse."

"He's a beautiful horse," Val said. "But not as beautiful as The Gray Ghost, of course."

In Val's mind, The Gray Ghost was absolutely perfect, even though he was fifteen years old and couldn't see very well. Val had always dreamed of having her own horse. When she had used all her savings to buy The Ghost from his owners, who were about to have him put to sleep, her dream had come true.

"Of course not," Jill agreed. "The Ghost is the most beautiful horse in the world — or in Essex, Pennsylvania, anyway."

"Vallie, you better put the chicken in the oven in about fifteen minutes," Erin said. "Three hundred and fifty degrees, remember. I'm going back down to the basement — I'm learning the main part in *Coppélia* and I have to practice real hard."

"I thought you were one of the townspeople, not Coppélia herself," Val said.

"I am," Erin told her cheerfully. "But if Donna Blum sprains her ankle or something before the recital, somebody will have to take her place. Besides, if I'm going to be a ballerina like Mommy was, I'll have to learn all the great roles sooner or later, and it might as well be sooner."

She danced off to the basement door and down the stairs.

Val looked after her little sister, smiling. "She *will* be, you know," she told Jill. "Erin's a wonderful ballet dancer. She's so graceful and delicate. Not like me. Erin's really got what it takes to be a real ballerina."

Jill rested her chin on one hand. "You're really lucky, Val," she said a little wistfully. "I mean, it was awful about your mother, but you still have Teddy and Erin and Doc. Things are always *happening* in this house! There's never a dull moment."

"You can say that again!" Val agreed as she took the chicken out of the refrigerator and put it into the oven, carefully adjusting the temperature. "Still, sometimes I envy you. It must be nice being an only child."

"Oh, yeah, it has its good points," Jill said. "I don't have to worry about taking care of little brothers and sisters, the way you do, and I love my mom and dad. But sometimes . . . well, sometimes, I wish my life was a little more *disorganized*, know what I mean?"

Val thought about that for a moment, then said, "Yeah, I guess I do. Hey, but listen, Jill, anytime you get tired of being the one and only, all you have to do is come over here. We'll disorganize you, all right!"

Just then Teddy burst into the kitchen, followed by Eric and Billy.

"Hey, Vallie, Eric's mom said okay but Billy's mom said no because his grandparents are coming for dinner. So Billy has to go, and is there any more lemonade? Because we're really thirsty, and Billy has to ride his bike all the way back home, and he'll pass out if he doesn't have something to drink. And Billy and Eric can come with us to the carnival. And the Eagles won!"

"Super!" Val said. "There's a little more lemonade — help yourselves."

"Thanks, Vallie," Teddy said, sloshing the last of the lemonade into Billy's glass. "Boy, I can't wait to go to the carnival. Carnivals are almost as much fun as circuses, only littler."

"Watch out, Teddy," Jill warned. "You're going to spill the lemonade, and it'll make a sticky, icky mess."

"Oh, Jill, what do *you* know? You're just a dumb girl," Teddy said, poking her in the arm.

"Oh, I am, am I?" Jill leaped up and began to tickle him in the ribs. Teddy yelped, squawked, and wriggled out of her grasp.

"No fair! Tickling isn't fair! Boy, having you around is just like having another sister!" he shouted.

"See what I mean?" Val said, laughing. "Want a little brother? He's all yours. Come on, Jill. The phone's free — you can call your folks."

Chapter 2

That Friday morning, Zefferelli's Kosmic Karnival appeared on the Essex fairgrounds at the north end of town. It was like magic, Val thought as she looked through the wrought-iron fence that surrounded the grounds on Friday afternoon after school. She'd made a big detour on her way to her job at Animal Inn just to see if the carnival had really arrived. On Thursday, the fairgrounds had been just a collection of empty buildings, deserted as it always was except for the one week in early September when the Middleton County Fair was held. But today, a huge Ferris wheel, merry-go-round, swing ride, Tilt-a-Whirl, and various other rides had sprung up, surrounded by booths for games of skill and chance, refreshment stands, and a big tent with a sign saying MENAGERIE off to one side. A red banner with the words ZEFFERELLI'S KOSMIC KARNIVAL was strung between the posts of the main gate, and posters were plastered on each gate post announcing a Demolition

Derby and trick motorcycle riding on the racetrack every night at eight.

Val knew that Doc wouldn't take them to see the Demolition Derby or the motorcycle riding, but that was all right with her. She hated seeing people doing daredevil stunts with beat-up old cars or fancy motorcycles while the audience roared and applauded every time a driver cracked up, or a rider flew through the air when his motorcycle went out of control. But Val certainly wouldn't have to see the Demolition Derby to enjoy herself at the carnival. Already she could picture how much fun she'd have taking Teddy and Erin around the fair. She could smell candy apples and cotton candy and popcorn with lots of butter, and another smell, one she couldn't put a name to, that meant "carnival."

She sniffed the air. Hot dogs, and big fat soft pretzels with lots of mustard, and Italian sandwiches with peppers and onions. Val's mouth watered, even though she wasn't really hungry. Suddenly she could hardly wait for Monday afternoon, when Doc had promised to take the whole gang — her, Jill, Toby, Erin, and her friend Olivia, Teddy, Eric, and Billy — to the carnival. She wished she could go in right now, but tomorrow was the official opening day. Besides, it wouldn't be any fun by herself. The great thing about going to a carnival was being with lots of family and friends.

And this year, Val just knew she'd win a prize with her pitching. She'd gotten much better. Last year, Erin had fallen in love with a big purple stuffed worm that Val had tried to win for her, but she hadn't been able to do it. But *this* year she would. She'd win the biggest, purplest, fattest stuffed worm there ever was!

Val glanced at her watch and groaned. If she didn't get going, she'd be late for her job at Animal Inn. Doc would understand — he always did — but Val didn't like to take advantage of the fact that she was Doc's daughter when she had a job to do.

"There's a parking place, Dad, right behind that car," Teddy shouted in Doc's ear on Monday afternoon. Doc Taylor had been circling around the fairgrounds with his vanful of eager children for what seemed like hours, though it was really only minutes.

"Good for you, Teddy," said Doc, easing the Animal Inn van into the vacant spot.

When he had parked the van, he turned to his eight charges and, focusing on Val, said, "Okay, guys, here's what we'll do. There are nine of us, so it's possible we may get separated as we wander around. Val — you, Jill, and Toby are the oldest. Each of you keep an eye on Erin, Olivia, Teddy, Eric, and Billy, and I'll keep an eye on everybody. If anyone gets lost, come to the front gate of the fairgrounds and *wait*. Got that? *Wait*. Do not move. If anybody's missing, I'll check out the front gate first thing. But in order to avoid getting lost, everybody stick close to everybody else. There are a lot of people here this afternoon, so it's possible somebody might get confused. *Do not panic*. Whatever happens, we'll find you."

"Got it, Dad," Val said, smiling. "Jill and Toby and I can handle it."

"Olivia and I will be just fine," Erin said. "We never get lost."

Olivia, a slender, dark-haired little girl who was in Erin's ballet class, nodded silently.

"We won't, either," Teddy put in. "Me and Eric and Billy'll stick closer than glue, right, guys?"

Eric and Billy nodded, beaming.

"Good. Then let's go."

Everybody piled out of the van and followed Doc to the main gates of the fairgrounds. As they passed through, the cheerful noise of the carnival assaulted their ears. The music from the merry-go-round, the cries of the barkers at the game booths, and the roar of the motors of the Ferris wheel and the other rides formed a blanket of sound that wrapped them up in excitement. Families wandered hand in hand from booth to booth, and crowds of teenagers headed for the most exciting and dangerous rides.

"We wanna go on the Tilt-a-Whirl, Dad," Teddy cried.

"The merry-go-round," Erin shouted.

"The Ferris wheel," added Val.

"One at a time," Doc said. He gave Teddy enough money to buy tickets for the Tilt-a-Whirl, and Erin enough to have a ride on the merry-go-round. But when he came to Val, she shook her head.

"I have my own money," she said proudly. "And so do Toby and Jill. We'll meet you back here in about fifteen minutes, okay?"

Doc cocked an eyebrow at her. "What makes you think I don't want to go on any of these rides?" he said.

Jill grabbed his hand. "Oh, Doc, want to come with us? Toby and Val can sit in one car, and you can sit with me in another one."

"Nope," Doc said with a smile. "I think I'll join Teddy and his pals on the Tilt-a-Whirl."

"All *right*!" Teddy cried. "Meet you after the ride's over, Vallie. And don't you dare go anywhere without us!"

Val laughed. "I won't. C'mon, Toby, Jill. We can all squeeze into one car on the Ferris wheel."

Val had always loved the Ferris wheel best of all the rides, at the fair or at the carnival. When she got to the top, she could see all over Middleton County, across the rolling Pennsylvania farmlands to the misty blue mountains beyond. It wasn't scary, like the other rides — except when she was sitting in a car with somebody who liked to swing the seat back and forth. That made her nervous. Toby tried it once, but she and Jill squealed in terror, so he stopped.

"Girls!" he muttered under his breath.

When the ride was over, Val, Jill, and Toby rejoined the rest of their gang. Everybody was by then "starvin' like Marvin," as Teddy often said, so they bought hot dogs, sausages, cotton candy, and candy apples, as well as soda and lemonade.

"Let's see the 'nagery," Teddy said. His face was covered with bright pink cotton candy. Val thought she ought to wipe it off, but she knew he'd be furious if she acted like a big sister, so she didn't.

Then she saw a booth with stuffed cats and baseballs.

"Can I try to win a prize?" she asked Doc.

"Why not? It's your money," Doc said, ruffling her hair.

Narrowing her eyes, Val plunked down some quarters on the counter. The attendant gave her three balls. Val picked one up in her hand, and realized the ball weighed nothing at all. How would she ever be able to knock down any of those figures with such a light ball?

"C'mon, little lady. Give it your best shot," said the man behind the counter.

Val gripped the ball, thinking of the Hamilton Raiders, her school's softball team. Zeroing in on the top of the first cat's head, she paused, then aimed and threw.

The cat dropped behind the counter.

Teddy, Erin, and their friends cheered.

"Atta girl, Vallie!" Doc said, beaming.

"Not bad — for a girl," said Toby.

Val looked at him with a scowl.

"Betcha can't do it again," he added.

"Oh, yeah? Watch this!" Val picked up the second ball, wound up, and threw. But she was so annoyed at Toby that she missed by a mile.

Everybody groaned — everybody, that is, except Toby. He just grinned. Val gritted her teeth and counted to ten, reminding heself that most of the time Toby was her very best friend, next to Jill, of course. Even though she knew that she wouldn't win first prize even if she knocked down the third cat, Val grabbed the last ball. She took careful aim, and gave it everything she had. The third cat disappeared behind the counter, to more cheers and applause from the Taylor crowd.

"Two out of three wins this supersonic plastic whistle, little lady," said the attendant, handing Val the whistle.

"Hey, that's neat, Vallie. If you don't want it, can I have it?" Teddy asked.

"Sure — be my guest," Val told him.

Teddy grabbed it and began blowing into it. The noise was deafening, and all the girls clapped their hands over their ears.

"How about giving it another try?" the attendant suggested. "You've got a great pitching arm there. You play softball, right?"

"That's right," Val said. Was it worth another dollar to try again? She glanced up at the shelves behind the cats and saw a beautiful turquoise plush unicorn with flowers twined around its horn. Erin was looking at it, too, an expression of longing on her heart-shaped face. It would be great to win the unicorn for Erin!

But before Val could dig out another dollar, Toby had stepped up. He put his money down and took three balls.

"Hey, these balls don't weigh anything," he said in surprise.

"I *know*," Val said sharply. "That's what makes it so hard."

"Strength, that's all it is," Toby muttered. "Boys are stronger than girls. Watch this!"

He stepped back, scuffed the ground with one sneakered foot, positioned himself, threw — and missed.

"Gee, Toby, what's wrong?" Teddy asked.

"Nothing's wrong," Toby said, scowling. "It was the wind. Didn't you feel that breeze? It blew the ball off course."

Val met Jill's eyes and stifled a giggle. "Oh, yes, Toby," she said sweetly. "It was almost a *hurricane*!"

"Very funny!" Toby mumbled. He picked up the second ball, aimed, and threw, knocking down one cat. "See that?" he said proudly.

"Sorry, fella — the cat didn't fall off the ledge, so it doesn't count," the attendant said cheerfully. "Looks like the little lady here's got you beat."

Toby's ears turned bright pink, the way they always did when he was embarrassed. Val didn't say a word. He threw the third ball, and this time he hit the cat square in the head, knocking it out of sight.

Everybody cheered for him, including Val.

"That was a real good throw, Toby," Teddy said.

"Thanks." Toby shoved his hands in his jeans pockets and turned away, ears flaming, head down.

Val followed him. "Toby?" she said softly.

"What?" Toby scowled at her.

"It *was* a good throw. It takes strength to throw that hard."

"Yeah — well, accuracy's important, too. You were good, Val, even though you're not as strong as me," he said, smiling a little.

"Thanks." Val grinned at him, and finally he grinned back.

"Say, let's ask Doc to take a turn. I bet he's better than either of us," Toby said.

Val nodded eagerly and went over to her father, who was helping Teddy pitch. Teddy didn't hit any of the cats, but the attendant gave him a balloon anyway.

"Dad, Toby and I want you to give it a try," Val said.

"Oh, yes, Daddy, do it!" Erin cried.

"Yeah, Dad, come on!" Teddy grabbed three more balls and thrust them at Doc. Doc rubbed his beard and raised one eyebrow (Val had tried for years to do that, but whenever she raised one, the other one shot up, too).

"That'll be a buck," the attendant said.

Doc reached into the hip pocket of his faded jeans and pulled out his wallet. "You got it," he said, putting down a dollar bill.

Doc picked up the first ball and weighed it in his hand. "Okay, here goes," he said.

The pitch was so fast that Val could hardly see it. A stuffed cat leaped off the ledge and fell down behind it.

"Way to go!" Teddy shouted.

He picked up the second ball. Again, he hit the cat dead center and knocked it off.

"Two out of three!" Val crowed. "Only one more!"

Doc tossed the third ball up and down a few times. Then he stared at the remaining cat, his eyes narrowed as Val's had been. He swung, pitched, and the last ball struck the stuffed cat on the top of the head, knocking it off the ledge.

Val, Toby, Jill, Erin, Olivia, Teddy, and Teddy's friends went wild. So did the people who had gathered around to watch.

"Hey, fella, you're one cool pitcher!" the attendant said. "Choice of the stand. Whaddya want — how about this AM-FM radio? Or the camera? Or the Walkman? Anything you want, it's yours."

Doc glanced at Val, and she nodded.

"I think I'd like the turquoise unicorn with the flowers," Doc said.

"You want it, you got it. Here you are!" The man grabbed the unicorn and shoved it at Doc. He took it, and turned to Erin. "This unicorn needs a good home," he said. "Think you can find room for it?"

"Oh, Daddy! For me?" Erin's eyes were wide and starry as she embraced the plush animal. "He's so beautiful! But you ought to take something *you* could use. Like the radio, or the camera. . . ."

"I have everything I need," Doc said, stroking Erin's shiny blonde hair. "He's yours. I don't imagine he'll eat much, and you won't have to walk him or provide him with a litter box. That's the kind of pet we need."

Erin, the unicorn clutched under one arm, threw her free arm around Doc and hugged him. "Thank you, Daddy. I love him already."

"I know," Doc said.

Next, they tossed darts at balloons and went around to every booth until each one of them had some kind of prize to take home. Finally, when they had gone on every ride that appealed to them, Val said, "Okay . . . let's go to the menagerie."

"That's what I've been saying for *ages*," Teddy shouted. "I want to see the animals!"

"You're on," said Doc, and led the way to the grubby-looking tent that housed Zefferelli's animals.

The minute they walked inside, Val cringed. It smelled terrible. There were cages ranged around the tent in which sleepy-looking animals lay, their eyes half closed. A mangy bear stared out at them from one cage. His fur was matted and he had a lot of bald spots. A tiger lay in another cage. The tiger was sleeping and paid no attention to the people who peered in at him. A young elephant munched at some wisps of hay, but its eyes were dull and lusterless.

"Dad, I don't like this," Val whispered, taking her father's hand. "Animals shouldn't *be* like this!"

"You're right, Vallie," Doc said. "We'll leave right away."

"Hey, Vallie, come look at this monkey!" Teddy was peering through the bars at a small capuchin monkey. A sign over its cage said GIGI. Gigi was huddled in a corner of its cage. Its eyes were bleary and filled with mucus. As Val looked at it, it looked back at her, and there was something in its beseeching gaze that wrung her heart.

"Dad, this animal is sick!" Val cried.

"Gigi has a cold, that's all. Gigi is usually a healthy animal. She makes the people laugh. But now, Gigi does not make the people laugh. The people feel sorry for her. How can I make money with a monkey the people feel sorry for?"

A sturdy, dark-haired man had come up next to Val and Doc.

"Gigi does not get better. I try everything I know, but Gigi will not be funny the way she used to be. I think I get rid of Gigi if she does not get well."

"Have you taken her to a vet?" Doc asked.

"No — no vet. We don't stay in one place long enough to take Gigi to a vet. You know a vet?" the little man asked.

"I *am* a vet," Doc said. "This monkey obviously has an upper respiratory infection. And she appears to be undernourished. Antibiotics and good food would fix her up in no time. Why don't you bring her to

Animal Inn? That's my veterinary clinic. It's right off the York Road, on Orchard Lane. We can give her what she needs to make her better."

"I will do that," the man said. "I will do that right away. Hey, you want to take a look at Little Leo? Little Leo is my lion cub. I bought him real cheap from a circus in New Jersey. The people like him because he is cute, but now he isn't cute anymore. He just lies there. He doesn't eat, or play, or do anything. Can you make him better, too?"

"Daddy, if you don't mind, Olivia and I are going outside," Erin said. "The smell in here is making us sick. And . . ." she glanced at the sturdy, dark-haired man and whispered in Doc's ear, "I can't stand to look at these poor animals!"

Doc nodded. "I know what you mean," he said. "We won't be long. Wait right outside the door, though."

"Okay," Erin said. She grabbed Olivia's hand. "Let's go, Olivia. Teddy, are you and Eric and Billy staying?"

Teddy made a face. "No way! I don't like this zoo at all!"

He and his friends trotted out of the tent after Erin and Olivia, and Jill joined them. Toby, however, stayed with Doc and Val.

Val went over to the dirty cage where Little Leo, the lion cub, was lying, and crouched down so she was at eye level with the animal. Little Leo was a very sad sight. He was even mangier than the bear, and so thin that Val could see all his ribs. He was probably about three or four months old, she guessed. Tears stung Val's eyes. How could anybody let a baby like this get so sick?

"This little guy looks like he's on his last legs," Toby said, scowling. "Don't you feed him?" he asked the menagerie man.

The man drew himself up to his full height, but since he wasn't very tall, the gesture wasn't very impressive.

"You ask if Tonio Zefferelli does not feed his animals? Sure, I feed them. I feed Little Leo all the time, but he won't eat. I feed him ground horsemeat, but he doesn't like it." Val shuddered at the thought.

There was a mound of brownish-gray mush in a cracked bowl in one corner of Little Leo's cage. It smelled awful. No wonder Little Leo wouldn't eat it, Val thought angrily. If he did, he'd be even sicker.

Doc came over and stood next to Toby and Val, looking down at the lion cub. "Mr. Zefferelli, Little Leo is just a cub. He needs a special diet — good, *fresh* meat, and plenty of milk, and vitamins. He may also have an infection, or possibly intestinal parasites. He needs medical attention immediately."

"You're right," Mr. Zefferelli said. "You take care of Little Leo, okay? You fix him up. I'll have my son Cesare bring him and Gigi to your hospital, and you make them well. We'll do it right now. The price does not matter. Whatever it costs, I'll pay." He strode to the rear of the tent, stuck his head out the flap, and yelled, "Hey, Cesare! Get your lazy bones over here! And bring the truck."

Val and Doc looked at each other helplessly. Animal Inn was officially closed today, but they couldn't turn away two animals as sick as the monkey and the lion cub.

"All right, Mr. Zefferelli," Doc said. "Tell your son to load Little Leo and Gigi into the truck. I'll get my van and wait for him at the main entrance to the fairgrounds. It's a dark blue van with 'Animal Inn Vet Van' on the side. He can't miss it. He can follow me to the clinic."

"Ah, Doctor, you are a good man. I knew that the minute I see you," said Mr. Zefferelli, grabbing Doc's hand and pumping it vigorously. "And tomorrow, I will come to your hospital myself, and you will tell me what to do for these poor beasts, and how much I pay."

Val, Toby, and Doc went out of the menagerie tent and collected Erin, Jill, Olivia, Teddy, Eric, and Billy. A few minutes later, they had all piled into the van, and Doc drove to the main entrance. Soon a rickety truck pulled up behind them, and a young man leaned out of the driver's side and waved. Doc drove off, closely followed by the truck.

"That was really disgusting," Jill said. "I never saw such a miserable bunch of animals in my entire life!"

"Me, neither," said Teddy. "You oughta get the Human Society after those people, Dad."

"That's the *Humane* Society, Teddy," his father corrected. "But you're right. Something should be done about people who treat animals so badly. Unfortunately, in a situation like this where the carnival is always moving from one town to another, it's hard to pin them down."

"Well, at least we'll be able to help Gigi and Little Leo," Val said. "And we can tell Mr. Zefferelli how to take care of them and the other animals."

Doc glanced over at her. His expression was solemn. "Yes, we can, Vallie. But there's no guarantee that he'll follow through. Still, we'll do our best. That's all we can do!"

Chapter 3

After Little Leo and Gigi had been moved into Animal Inn, Doc drove Teddy and his friends, Erin, Olivia, and Jill back to town, then came back to examine the lion cub and the monkey. Mike Strickler, the little old man who took care of Animal Inn's patients at night and on Sundays and Mondays, was fascinated by his new charges.

"We've never had any of them before," he told Val, his eyes sparkling. "Don't know as I've ever had anything to do with monkeys or lions before. But when I was a kid, way back before you were born, there used to be organ grinders who had monkeys in funny little suits. Those monkeys were real smart — they used to hold a tin cup in their little paws, and they'd run around to all the people who were listening to the organ grinder play his music, and they'd shove that cup at you so you'd drop in some money."

Doc was examining Gigi as Mike spoke. "It's just as I suspected," he said. "A severe upper respiratory infection and malnutrition. A course of antibiotics ought to do the trick, along with a nutritious diet. I'll give Gigi a shot now, and when Mr. Zefferelli picks her up tomorrow, I'll give him instructions on the monkey's medication and food."

Gigi had behaved herself very well during the examination, and now she looked up at Val and reached out her skinny little arms. Val picked her up and held her close.

"You're going to be fine, Gigi," she said. "You'll stay here tonight, and tomorrow you'll be back with all your friends at the carnival. . . ." Her voice trailed off. Val couldn't think of anything worse than sending Gigi back to her filthy, smelly home.

"Give her to me, Vallie," Mike said. "I got a real nice cage for her, right next to Mr. Mumma's cat. Don't know if monkeys and cats speak the same language, but I guess they can learn."

"What about Little Leo?" Toby asked. "Are you going to examine him now, Doc?"

"I sure am," Doc said. He looked down at the lion cub lying on the stainless steel table. "As soon as I wash up, I'm going to check him out and run some blood tests."

While Doc scrubbed at the sink, Val stroked Little Leo's scruffy head. He opened one foggy eye, then closed it again. The lion was supposed to be the king of beasts, Val thought sadly, but this cub didn't look in the least like a prince. She thought about a TV documentary she had seen about African lions. The lions she'd seen were big, fierce animals who ruled the plains and were incredibly beautiful. They had radiated health and strength. And at the zoo she'd seen fat, happy lion cubs playing like over-sized kittens. Poor Little Leo! Unless Doc could find out what was wrong with him, he'd never grow up to be a king of the jungle — or of anything else.

"Hold on to him, Toby, just in case he decides to fight back," Doc said.

Toby did as he was told, but there didn't seem to be any fight left in Little Leo at all.

Doc carefully examined the lion cub from head to tail, peering into its mouth and ears, gently pressing its abdomen (Little Leo growled at this), and listening to the animal's lungs and heartbeat. Then he took some blood samples. At last he said, "Well, I won't be sure until I get the results of the tests, but it seems pretty clear that this little fellow is half-starved, like Gigi, and he probably has a bacterial infection from the bad meat he's been fed. Good thing he hasn't been eating much of that garbage, or he probably wouldn't have lasted as long as he has."

"He's going to be all right, isn't he, Dad?" Val asked anxiously. "He isn't going to die?"

"He'll be all right if we can convince Zefferelli to follow the course of treatment I prescribe and feed him decent food," Doc replied. "Now I'm going to give him some multivitamin shots, an antibiotic to insure against infection, and we'll start him on a special diet."

"Teddy's right," Val said. "We ought to call the Humane Society. You're a member of the board here, Dad. Can't you make them do something about the way Mr. Zefferelli treats his animals?"

"Honey, it's like I said before. It's almost impossible to force an outfit like Zefferelli's Kosmic Karnival to mend their ways because they're constantly on the move. There's no way to keep track of them."

Doc gave Little Leo an injection and discarded the syringe.

"But the carnival's going to be in town for one more day," Toby said. "Couldn't you get the sheriff or somebody to give them a summons?"

"I intend to call Sheriff Weigel as soon as I'm through here," said Doc. "But the federal Animal Welfare Act is very poorly enforced, and people tend to close their eyes to problems of animal health."

"That ain't right," Mike said. "Some of my best friends are animals. The way I figure it is, animals are just like people, only they don't pay taxes and they don't vote, so the government doesn't care about them. If Leo here was a citizen, you can bet somebody would pay attention to him."

"You're right, Mike," Doc said. "So it's up to

people like us — you, and Vallie and Toby and me — to speak for them. All life is valuable. If I didn't believe that, I wouldn't have become a veterinarian."

Little Leo struggled weakly in Toby's arms, then lay still again.

"When Mr. Zefferelli comes to pick up Leo and Gigi tomorrow, I'll supply him with enough medication and food to last for at least a week. He can renew the prescription wherever they play next."

"*If* he'll do it," Val said.

"If he'll do it," Doc agreed with a sigh. "All right — that's all I can do for now. Take him into intensive care, Toby."

Toby lifted the groggy lion cub and carried him into the room where the sickest animals were tended to. Mike had prepared a soft bed for Little Leo in the largest cage. Like all the other cages at Animal Inn, this one was sparkling clean, with a floor of sturdy wire mesh fine enough to prevent an animal's foot from slipping through. The cushion Mike had put down was filled with cedar shavings and smelled fresh and sweet.

Toby gently put Little Leo down, and Val reached in and patted him, then tickled him under the chin the way she often did to Cleveland.

"You're going to be a king when you grow up," she told him softly. "So what if you're kind of scrawny right now? Pretty soon you'll be strong and healthy again, and you'll learn how to roar, and you'll grow a wonderful, big, bushy mane, and long, sharp teeth, and everybody will be scared to death of you."

Little Leo looked up at her, then lowered his head until it rested on his paws. His eyes slowly closed.

"The king of beasts," Val said. "Don't you forget it, Little Leo. You rest now. I'll see you tomorrow."

Then Val moved on to the cage where Gigi sat. The little monkey was gripping the wire mesh of the cage door, peering sadly out at Val. Val stuck one finger through the mesh, and Gigi immediately grasped it with both paws — like two tiny human hands, Val thought. She wondered how old Gigi was. From all her reading about animals, Val knew that monkeys could live for as long as thirty years. But in spite of Gigi's mangy, sorrowful appearance and the fact that she was so thin, Val was sure she was much younger than she looked, maybe only four or five years old.

"Don't worry, Gigi," Val said softly. "You're going to feel much better in the morning. Mike will take real good care of you."

From the next cage, Mr. Mumma's cat, Whiskers, let out a plaintive mew. Whiskers had gotten into a fight with another cat and was recuperating from his wounds.

"Sorry, Whiskers. I didn't mean to ignore you," Val said. "Meet your new neighbor. Her name is

Gigi, and she's a monkey. Bet you've never seen one before." She opened the door of Whiskers' cage and scratched the cat under its chin. Whiskers closed his eyes and purred.

"I wonder if cats and monkeys *do* speak the same language," Val mused aloud. "Probably not."

Just then Gigi, who was feeling neglected, started to chatter loudly. Whiskers stopped in mid-purr. He arched his back and all his tiger-striped fur stood on end, making him look twice his normal size. He glared over at Gigi and hissed.

"Never mind, Whiskers," Val soothed. "Calm down, Gigi. It would be nice if you two could be friends, but if you can't, you only have to put up with each other for a little while. Gigi will be going home tomorrow."

She sighed. Home. She hated to think of Gigi going back to that dirty, smelly tent. It was no fit home for any animal, much less sick ones like the monkey and Little Leo.

"Good night, Whiskers," she said, closing and latching the cat's cage. "Sleep tight, Gigi."

But Val knew that *she* wouldn't sleep well that night, worrying about what would happen to Gigi and Little Leo once they left Animal Inn.

As she came back into the treatment room, she heard Toby talking to Doc.

"Doc, are you really going to let those Zefferellis

take Little Leo and Gigi back to the carnival tomorrow?" Toby asked.

"I'm afraid so," said Doc as he washed up at the sink in the treatment room. "The animals belong to them. There's no legal way I can keep them here, even if I can persuade Sheriff Weigel to investigate the conditions in the menagerie."

"I bet they won't even give them the medication on schedule," Val said. "And as for a special diet, forget it! Those people don't really care about their animals. They only want to make money from them. What did it cost for all of us to go into that stinky tent and look at those poor, miserable things?"

"Two dollars for adults and a dollar apiece for you youngsters," Doc told her.

Toby immediately pulled out his wallet and fished out a dollar bill. "Here, Doc. That's my share. It's not fair that you had to pay for all of us. You know what I think? I think we oughta go back and tell Mr. Zefferelli we want a refund. We could even make signs and picket the menagerie!" he said excitedly. "We could keep people from coming in, and if he couldn't make any more money on his animals, maybe he'd . . . he'd. . . ."

"He'd get the law on you, that's what he'd do," Mike said. "And if them poor critters weren't making any more money for him, I betcha he'd sell 'em for dog food!"

"Oh, Mike!" Val wailed.

"No picketing," Doc said sternly. "It won't do any good." He handed the dollar back to Toby. "Thanks, Toby, but this little excursion isn't going to bankrupt me." He turned to Mike. "Mike, you keep a close eye on Gigi and Leo. Antibiotics every four hours around the clock — I've written down who gets what when. And make sure they both get their liquid formula at the proper time."

"You don't need to tell me that, Doc," Mike said, bristling. "How long I been your night man at Animal Inn, huh? Have I ever missed a medication or a feeding? Have I?"

Doc shook his head, smiling.

"I may be gettin' on in years," Mike grumbled as he finished scrubbing the examining table, "but I haven't lost my marbles yet."

Val said quickly, "Mike, we know that. You're the best, the very best!"

"You bet I am," Mike said. "And just because them new patients aren't sheep, or cows, or dogs, or cats don't mean that I don't know what to do." Then he grinned at Val. "I'm lookin' forward to havin' a long conversation with that monkey. Never talked to a monkey before. She's probably got some interestin' stories to tell."

Val laughed. "Mike, you're even more of an animal nut than I am! I talk to them all the time, but so far, they've never talked back."

"That's 'cause you don't listen close," Mike said with a twinkle in his eye.

"I do, too," Val told him. "And sometimes I really think The Ghost understands what I say, and I understand what *he* says — kind of. And I talk to Cleveland a lot." Her big, fat orange cat always had a lot to say, usually complaints about the dogs and about the fact that his milk bowl was sometimes empty.

"Well, you listen real good to that horse of yours," Mike said. "The Gray Ghost's one smart animal and he loves you a lot."

"And I love *him* a lot," said Val. She glanced up at her father. "Dad, do I have time to check on The Ghost? There's an apple in the refrigerator that I'd like to give him before we go."

"Sure, go ahead," Doc said. "Toby, want a lift?"

"I wouldn't mind," Toby admitted. "I'll finish cleaning the waiting room, then I'll be ready to go."

Val took the apple out of the refrigerator in the treatment room and hurried off to visit The Ghost.

He nickered softly when he saw her, stretching his glossy dapple-gray neck over the door of his stall in the barn. Val broke the apple in half (a trick Doc had taught her — you grasped the apple and twisted, and it came apart in two neat sections), and The Ghost delicately lifted first one half, then the other from her outstetched palm.

"We have some new patients in intensive care, Ghost," Val told him, rubbing between his ears. "A monkey and a baby lion. Isn't that weird? They belong to Zefferelli's carnival, and they're both in pretty bad shape because nobody's taken care of them. And tomorrow, they have to go back to the carnival. I'm worried about them, because I don't think the carnival people care enough to give them their medicine so they can get better. But Dad says we have to let them go. They don't belong to us, after all."

The Ghost nodded and butted his head against Val's chest.

"Yes, I guess you're right," she said. "There's nothing we can do. Oh, Ghost, it's so unfair! If we could keep them here for a while, I know they'd be fine. But when they go back, I'm sure they're going to die. And there's not a thing I can do about it."

"Vallie, we're ready to go," Doc called from the doorway.

"Okay, Dad, I'm coming."

Val gave The Ghost one last pat. "See you tomorrow after school. We'll have a ride. Sleep well, Ghost." She wrapped her arms around the horse's neck, pressing her cheek against him. "And tomorrow, I'll bring you some carrots."

The Ghost whickered softly. He *did* understand what she'd said, Val was sure.

Chapter 4

As soon as Val and Doc got home that evening, Doc called Sheriff Weigel about investigating conditions in Zefferelli's menagerie. Val waited impatiently to hear what the sheriff had to say, but from what she could hear of her father's end of the conversation, she could tell that there was a problem. The minute Doc hung up, Val asked, "What did he say, Dad? Will he do it?"

"No, he won't," Doc told her, rubbing his salt-and-pepper beard the way he always did when he was upset. "He says it's not his job. Situations like this are handled by the Humane Society of the United States Captive Wildlife Department, and he's not authorized to do anything about it."

"Oh, dear!" Val groaned. "What do we do now?"

"I'll call some of the other Humane Society board members and ask them to come with me tomorrow to the carnival. We'll speak to Mr. Zefferelli and try to make him understand that he has to improve his care of the animals or he'll be prosecuted. That may do some good."

Val sighed. "Maybe. I don't think Mr. Zefferelli's a *bad* man, Dad. But he just doesn't understand that animals have rights, too."

"Few people do," Doc said wearily. "I hate allowing Gigi and Leo to go back to the carnival as much as you do, but when Zefferelli or his son shows up tomorrow, we'll have to let them take the animals and hope that they'll take proper care of them when they leave town."

"*I* think Mr. Zefferelli *is* a bad man," Teddy said. He had been listening to Val and Doc's conversation as he lay in front of the TV, watching a videocassette of yesterday's football game. "If he was a *good* man, he wouldn't let his zoo be so stinky and awful! I thought I was gonna throw up and so did Billy and Eric. I could hardly eat my soft pretzel with mustard after we went out of that tent."

"But you managed somehow, didn't you?" Val said, grinning in spite of herself.

"It wasn't easy," Teddy told her. "And I shared it with Eric and Billy."

He scrambled to his feet. "That reminds me — I'm starved!" He charged into the kitchen. "What're we having for dinner, Vallie?"

Doc began dialing the number of one of the Humane Society board members, and Val scooped up Cleveland, who had been weaving in and out between her legs, demanding to be picked up and cuddled. "You're hungry, too, aren't you?" Val asked the cat, and Cleveland purred and rubbed his head under her chin.

"Okay, okay. You don't have to cuddle me to death," Val said. "Your milk bowl's empty, right?"

Rrrrow! said Cleveland.

Val slung him over her shoulder and headed for the kitchen, and Jocko and Sunshine trotted after her. They knew that when Cleveland got a treat, they'd be given something good, too — maybe a biscuit, or a bone.

Val thought about Gigi and Little Leo, so thin and sick, in their cages at Animal Inn. Mike would see that they got their medicine and their special liquid diet, and he'd talk to them and make them feel at home. But what would happen to them tomorrow when they went back to the carnival? Would anybody care about them at all?

"They're gone."

Val stared at Doc, not knowing what he was talking about. She had just arrived at Animal Inn after school the next day.

"Who's gone? What do you mean?" she asked.

"Zefferelli's Kosmic Karnival. I went with Mr. Haines and Mrs. Flood to the fairgrounds first thing this morning, and the carnival was gone. There was nothing left but a lot of garbage littering the grounds. Everything was gone."

"Everything?" Val repeated, stunned. "The Ferris wheel, and the merry-go-round, and. . . ."

"Everything," Doc said. "They did a moonlight flit. They must have packed up last night and moved on, when everybody was sleeping."

Val couldn't believe it. "But they *can't*! Their posters said they'd be there until tonight!"

"They lied," Doc told her. "And nobody knows where they've gone."

"And they didn't pick up Gigi and Leo, either," Toby put in.

"Oh, wow!" Val was almost too amazed to speak. Finally she said,"Can't we chase them down? They can't just disappear like that!"

"But they have," Doc said.

"You know, Doc," Toby said, his eyes lighting up with excitement, "now they've really done something illegal! They cut out without paying for their animals' treatment. Sheriff Weigel will have to do something now!"

"I've already spoken to him," Doc told Toby. "And he said that since Zefferelli left the animals here, I don't have a case."

"That's nuts," Val cried. "It doesn't make any sense!"

"The idea is that Leo and Gigi are valuable property that can be sold to pay off the debt," Doc said with a half-smile.

"Valuable property!" Val echoed. "A lion cub who's so skinny and sick he can hardly stand up, and a mangy little monkey with an awful cold? You'd have to pay somebody to take them away!"

"Vallie, *I* know that and *you* know that and so does Toby," Doc said, "but the law doesn't know that, and Sheriff Weigel represents the law in Essex. He's not about to send anyone out hunting for the carnival when, according to the letter of the law, they haven't done anything wrong."

"Oh, boy," Toby sighed. "Val's right. That's the craziest thing I ever heard of."

"Well, there's one thing I'm happy about," Val said. "At least I won't have to worry about who's going to take care of Little Leo and Gigi when they go back to the menagerie. I could hardly sleep last night, thinking about them. They would have died for sure! And now we can take care of them ourselves, and feed them, and. . . ."

"And then what?" Doc asked gently. "We can't keep them forever, Vallie. Sooner or later, they'll have to leave. As a matter of fact, I'm faced with a big problem right now. There are four cages in intensive care. Leo and Gigi are in two of them, and Whiskers is in the third. That leaves only one cage empty, and Mrs. Wexler is on her way here this very minute with Frederick, her cocker spaniel. From what she tells me, he may have hookworm. I'll need a cage for him. Then there's Mr. Billings' cat. I saw her last week, remember, Vallie?"

Val nodded.

"Frisky isn't responding to the medication I prescribed. I'll need to keep her here for a few days, run some more tests. She'll need a cage, too. We just don't have enough space."

"How's Gigi doing?" Val asked. "She was pretty sick, but not as weak as Leo. Maybe we could put her somewhere else."

"There isn't anywhere else," Toby said. "We're full up."

"If Gigi were completely recovered," Doc said, "I'd take her to the Humane Society, although they're pretty cramped for space as well. There's no room at the shelter to keep an animal in isolation, and we can't risk Gigi spreading her infection to all those other animals."

Suddenly Val had an idea. "Dad," she said eagerly, "why don't we take her home with us?" Before Doc could object, she continued, "I could keep her in my room, and I'd see that she gets her medication regularly, and I'd feed her the special formula. And Teddy and Erin would love her."

"Val, you're out of your tree!" Toby groaned.

"Remember what happened when Teddy brought home that ferret? Mrs. Racer almost blew her top."

"I'm afraid it's out of the question, Vallie," Doc said firmly. "Toby's right. We can't put an extra burden on Mrs. Racer. She works very hard taking care of the house, and all of us, not to mention two dogs, one cat, Teddy's hamsters, Erin's canary, the rabbits, the chickens, and the duck."

"But Dad, Mrs. Racer *doesn't* take care of our pets. *We* do," Val reminded him. "And like I said, I'd keep Gigi in my room. Mrs. Racer wouldn't even know she was there, honest! And the reason she didn't like Frank was that she thought he was a weasel, and Mrs. Racer hates weasels."

"She also wasn't too happy about Frank stealing her cookies and running all over her kitchen," Doc said. "Teddy promised to keep Frank in his room, too, remember? But it just didn't work out."

The intercom in the treatment room buzzed, and they heard the voice of Pat Dempwolf, Doc's receptionist.

"Doc Taylor, Mrs. Wexler and Frederick are here, and Frederick looks real sick. Can you see him now?" she asked.

"Yes, Pat, in just a minute," Doc answered.

"There are several other patients waiting, too," Pat added. "Will you have time to see them or should I reschedule their appointments?"

"No, don't do that. I'll see them all." Doc turned to Val and Toby. "Val, bring Frederick in here. I'll look at him right away. Toby, you can deliver the medicine for Mr. Paxton's sheep on your bike."

"But, Dad, about Gigi . . ." Val began, but Doc cut her off.

"Vallie, we'll discuss it later. Right now, I've got to take care of a very sick cocker spaniel."

"Yes, Dad." Val sighed and hurried into the waiting room. There had to be some way to persuade Doc to let her bring Gigi home. But how?

It was almost six o'clock by the time Doc had tended to the last patient of the day. Besides Frederick Wexler and Frisky Billings, a third animal had been admitted to intensive care — a scarlet macaw named Crackers with an advanced case of parrot fever.

"Maybe we could put Whiskers in a crate and cover it with chicken wire," Toby suggested. "Then Frisky could go into Whiskers' cage and Frederick could go in the empty one."

"We're still short one cage," Doc said. "We can't just let Crackers fly around loose."

"Dad," said Val, "if we took Gigi with us, Crackers could have her cage. I'd clean it out myself with lots of disinfectant so there wouldn't be any of Gigi's germs left."

Doc sighed. "I give up. All right, we'll take Gigi.

Toby, you'll have to dig up something to use for a perch for Crackers — we have so few bird patients that I don't have proper housing for a parrot."

"Hooray!" Val cried. "I can't wait to see Teddy's and Erin's faces when we bring Gigi in!"

"And I *can* wait to see Mrs. Racer's," Doc mumbled. "We'll have to make it very clear to her that Gigi is only a temporary guest, not a new member of the family. And, until we're sure she's not contagious, try to keep her away from the other animals at home." He began washing up at the sink. "Mike should be here any minute. I'll give him his instructions on caring for our new patients. Vallie, after you clean Gigi's cage, don't forget to take her medication and formula from the refrigerator."

"I won't," Val promised.

In the intensive care unit, Gigi sat huddled in a corner of her cage, her small face looking sad. When she saw Val, she made a few sorrowful noises.

"Guess what, Gigi?" Val said. "You're coming home with me! You'll love it at our house. We don't have any other monkeys for you to play with, but as soon as you're better, you'll make friends with Jocko and Sunshine — they're our dogs — and my cat, Cleveland. And you'll get better real fast, you'll see."

Little Leo, in his cage, rumbled in his throat, and Val went over to him. "Was that the beginning of a roar?" she asked. "Or was it a purr? Do lions purr,

I wonder? I wonder what Cleveland would think of *you*. I wish you could come home with me, too, but I had enough trouble getting Dad to let me take Gigi."

Little Leo rumbled again, then rolled over and went back to sleep. Val gently lifted the monkey out, wrapped her in a small blanket, and put her down on the one chair in the room. Then she set to work scrubbing out Gigi's cage.

After Toby had installed a makeshift perch, Doc brought Crackers the macaw in. Crackers was very beautiful, with his bright red and green feathers, but Val thought he didn't look very happy. She hoped his owner had brought him to Animal Inn in time, because parrot fever could be fatal.

"Hey, whatcha got there, Val? That the macaw?" Mike asked, peering in at the bird. "Well, whaddya know! A lion, a monkey, and now a parrot. Maybe we oughta start a circus. How you doing, fella?"

The macaw cocked its head and looked at Mike out of one bleary eye.

"Shut up! Get lost!" it croaked.

"Well, I'll be — !" Mike said. "That's not very friendly-like. Don't you have anything nice to say?"

Val and Toby couldn't help giggling when Crackers replied, "Get lost! Shut up!"

Mike put his face closer to the cage and stared eye-to-eye with the bird. "I know you're sick, so I guess that makes you kinda irritable, but I'm not going to shut up, and I'm not going to get lost, so you just better get used to the idea," he said.

"Fiddlesticks," said Crackers, and closed his eyes.

"This is going to be a real interesting evening," Mike said, grinning at Toby and Val. "But don't you worry. By tomorrow morning, me and this parrot will be best pals, you wait and see."

Still laughing, Val picked up Gigi, who had sat patiently in the chair, half asleep, all this time.

" 'Night, Mike," she said. "And good luck!"

In the treatment room, she took Gigi's medicine out of the refrigerator, then joined Doc outside Animal Inn. As Toby mounted his bike, he said, "You might need some luck, too, Val. I bet I'll hear Mrs. Racer explode all the way over at the farm."

Val got into the car, still cradling Gigi in her arms. "Don't be silly, Toby. Who could object to a poor, quiet little thing like Gigi?"

Doc gave her a wry look. "Three guesses, and the first two don't count," he said.

Val waved out the window at Toby as Doc's car pulled away. She was beginning to be afraid that maybe Doc and Toby were right. Val loved Mrs. Racer, as did all the Taylors, and she didn't want to upset her. As Doc often said, Mrs. Racer had a lot to put up with. Maybe Gigi would be the last straw.

Chapter 5

"What've you got there, Vallie? It looks like a baby!" cried Erin as Val came into the house. She had wrapped Gigi up in a little bundle, covering even the monkey's head.

"A baby? Did somebody bring a *baby* to Animal Inn?" Teddy asked, running over to look.

"Who's got a baby? Doc, you didn't go and adopt a child!" Mrs. Racer came out of the kitchen, wiping her hands on her apron and tucking a stray strand of silver hair under the little white cap she wore, known as a prayer covering.

"No, no, no!" Doc laughed. "If everyone will quiet down for a minute, I'll explain. Or rather, Vallie will. It's her project."

"What is it? What's in the blanket if it's not a baby?" Erin asked, standing on tiptoe to get a closer peek.

Slowly and carefully, Val removed the blanket from Gigi's head.

"It's a monkey! It's that monkey from the carnival, isn't it, Vallie?" Teddy said. "But what's it doing here? I thought those carnival people were going to pick it up today."

"They were supposed to, but they skipped town. They also left Gigi and Little Leo the lion cub back at Animal Inn," Doc said. "We ran out of space, so I agreed that we could bring Gigi here for a few days until she recovers." He glanced at Mrs. Racer. "Don't worry, Mrs. Racer," he said quickly. "She won't be any trouble. She's sick and she'll stay in Vallie's room. You won't even know she's in the house."

"She won't be here for very long," Val added. "Just until she gets well and we can find a home for her." Anxiously, she waited for the housekeeper's reaction. Mrs. Racer had had a royal fit when Teddy had brought home Frank the ferret.

Mrs. Racer came over and looked down at Gigi's little wrinkled white face. Then she stretched out one hand and Gigi brought out a paw from under the blanket, seizing one of Mrs. Racer's fingers. Slowly, a smile spread over the old woman's face.

"You know," she said, "this here monkey reminds me of my little grandson Johnnie when he was born. That's m'son Henry's oldest boy. He was so little and skinny, everybody said he was a little monkey. He's twenty-three now and he don't look like a monkey anymore, but when he was a baby. . . ."

Val and Doc looked at each other, and both relaxed.

"Then you don't mind having Gigi stay for a while?" Val asked hopefully.

"Why should I mind?" Mrs. Racer replied. "The poor thing's sick and it needs good care. Whatever made you think I'd mind?"

"You minded Frank, all right," Teddy put in.

"Oh, that was because I hate weasels," Mrs. Racer told him. "But I like monkeys — or at least I like this one. Never knew any other monkey real well, but she's kind of cute."

"Well, then, that's settled," Doc said, smiling. "Vallie, you'd better take Gigi upstairs. Teddy and Erin, how about finding something she can use for a bed?"

"There's an empty carton down in the basement that I've been saving for something special," Teddy said. "This is pretty special, all right. I'll go get it right now."

"And we can put an old blanket in the bottom so it'll be nice and soft," Erin said.

Teddy dashed off for the basement and Erin headed upstairs to get the blanket, followed by Val holding Gigi.

"We really lucked out this time," she whispered into Gigi's ear. "Welcome to the Taylors'!"

* * *

"A monkey? You really have a monkey at your house?" Sarah Jones asked Val the next day at school. "Boy, Val, are you lucky! My folks won't even let me have a cat. They're afraid of germs."

"Then they'd *really* be afraid of Gigi," Val said. "She's got a very bad cold, but there wasn't room to keep her at Animal Inn because we had a lot of animals that were much sicker, so we brought her home."

"Honestly, Val," said Lila Bascombe, wrinkling her nose, "I'll never understand you. First you buy an ancient horse that's going blind, and now it's a horrible, sick monkey from that tacky carnival. I think it's disgusting!"

Val gritted her teeth. Lila Bascombe was the only person in the world whom Val really disliked, and she knew Lila disliked her, too. Lila had never forgiven Val for getting her into trouble with her parents not long ago, even though it was trouble Lila richly deserved. Ever since, Lila had been nastier than usual to Val, and Val knew that it was only a matter of time before Lila managed to get her revenge. The question was, when and how?

But she controlled her anger, and said, "I'm going to be a vet, Lila, so if there's a sick animal, I have to take care of it. And I don't think Gigi's disgusting at all. I just feel sorry for her and I want to make her well."

Lila rolled her eyes. "Oh, gimme a break!" she groaned. "The Florence Nightingale of Hamilton Junior High."

"Oh, dry up, Lila," Jill snapped. "Just because you don't care about anything but yourself doesn't mean that everyone's that way."

Before Lila could shoot back a reply, the bell rang, and the girls hurried off to English class.

English was one of Val's two favorite subjects. The other was biology. She was Ms. Lessing's star pupil in biology and one of Mr. Steele's best students in English.

"Class, I have an announcement to make," Mr. Steele said when everybody was seated. "The local branch of the Humane Society is sponsoring an essay contest at Hamilton. The subject is the responsibility of humans for our animal friends. The essay must be no more than one thousand words, and first prize is fifty dollars. I am assigning this to everyone. The deadline is a week from Friday. The winning essay will be printed in *The Essex Gazette*. Anyone have any questions?"

Dave Henderson's hand shot up. "Typewritten or handwritten?" he asked.

"Typewritten, ideally," Mr. Steele said. "But if you don't type and can't get anyone to type it for you, handwritten is acceptable, provided it's legible."

Now Lila raised her hand. "A thousand words

is awfully long," she complained. "Couldn't it be a little shorter — like two hundred fifty?"

Mr. Steele shook his head. "Sorry, Lila. I didn't make the rules. One thousand it is. I'm sure you'll have no trouble once you get going." He looked over at Val and smiled. "And, Val Taylor, remember — *only* a thousand words. Knowing how strongly you feel on the subject, I'm sure you could write a book. But restrain yourself, okay?"

Val smiled back. "I'll do my best."

Several other students had questions, but Val wasn't paying attention. She was lost in daydreams of what she would do with the prize money if she won. There was a beautiful bridle she'd seen in Bradford's tack shop. She longed to buy it for The Ghost, because the one he had was kind of worn. But it was more important, she knew, to save every cent she could to pay for the operation that might save The Ghost's sight. He had developed cataracts in both eyes, and if they were not removed, he would go completely blind. Doc knew of a veterinary surgeon in Philadelphia who could perform the delicate operation, but it was very expensive. He had told Val that if she could save up half the money, he would contribute the rest. Every week Val deposited some of her salary from Animal Inn in her savings account, but she still had a long way to go. If she could add fifty dollars, it would help a lot. When she had bought The Ghost, she had saved his life. Now she hoped she could save his sight.

"If I win," she heard Lila saying loudly to her friend Courtney, "I'm going to buy this great dress I saw in Brenda's Boutique. It's pale green, and it'll bring out the color of my eyes."

"That ought to make Eric Whiteside sit up and take notice," Courtney said. Eric was president of the eighth-grade class at Hamilton Junior High. Lila always had at least two boys she was interested in, and now that she was breaking up with Jeff Willard, she had her eye on Eric. Boy crazy, Jill called her, and Val agreed.

"And I *will* win, just you wait and see," Lila said smugly.

Val scowled. Much as she disliked Lila, she had to admit that Lila was very good in English. She'd even had articles published in the school paper. But what did Lila know or care about animals? Nothing, that's what.

"You're going to win, Val, I just know you are," Jill whispered. "It makes me sick the way Lila brags all the time!"

"Me, too," Val whispered back.

She'd start working on her essay tonight after supper. And it would be the very best thing she'd ever written. She just had to win the contest, for The Ghost's sake!

When Val came home that evening after working at Animal Inn, she hurried straight up the stairs to see how Gigi was doing. Mrs. Racer had told her that she didn't have to worry about giving the monkey her midday medication — Mrs. Racer would do it for her. Val still couldn't get over the housekeeper's reaction to Gigi. When she'd told Toby that Mrs. Racer actually liked the monkey because it reminded her of her first grandson, Toby had whooped with laughter.

"Boy, I'd like to see him now!" he said. "Wonder if he swings from the trees like Tarzan the apeman?"

"He does *not*!" Val said indignantly. "I've seen him and he's perfectly normal." She paused. "But come to think of it, the last time I saw him, he was eating a banana."

That set them both off into giggles, and Doc had to remind them sternly to tend to their chores.

Val opened her bedroom door very quietly and tiptoed over to Gigi's carton-bed. She peered inside. No Gigi!

"Gigi?" Val called. "Gigi, where are you? Are you playing hide-and-seek?"

She listened very carefully for any sound that

might tell her where the monkey was hiding, but she didn't hear a thing. So Val began to search — under her bed, behind her desk, in a bureau drawer that was half opened, in her closet. She even looked into the wastebasket, but there was no sign of Gigi.

Now Val was beginning to get worried. Maybe somebody had opened her door, and Gigi was hiding somewhere in the rest of the house. Or what if she'd managed to climb out the window? Val was sure she'd closed it when she left that morning. Yes, it was still closed. Thank goodness! She'd had visions of a sick little monkey sitting in a tree somewhere, lost and frightened.

Val went out into the hall. "Gigi! Gigi, where are you?" she shouted.

"Vallie, in here," Erin called from her room.

Val stuck her head in the door, and saw Erin sitting on the floor beside her canopied doll bed. In the bed was Gigi, the ruffled bedspread drawn up to her chin. Her big dark eyes were much brighter than they'd been that morning, Val noticed. The little monkey looked so funny lying there that Val burst out laughing.

"So that's where she went!" she cried when she could speak. "I thought maybe she'd run away. Did you bring her in here, Erin?"

"Don't be mad, Vallie," Erin said. "I came home from school and helped Mrs. Racer give Gigi her medicine and some of her formula, and then she looked so lonely that I brought her to my room. She just exactly fits in Elizabeth's bed, see? And since I'm really too old to play with dolls anymore, I thought I'd let Gigi use it for a while."

"I'm not mad, Erin. I was just worried, that's all."

Val sat down beside the doll bed, and Gigi immediately scrambled out and into Val's arms, chattering happily. Her nose was hardly running at all. She even looked a little fatter, Val thought, though she knew that was impossible after only one day of treatment and proper diet.

"She's lots better," Erin said. "Olivia came over for a while, and I let her visit Gigi. Olivia's nice and quiet, so I knew she wouldn't get Gigi all upset. But then Teddy and Billy wanted to come in and play with her, and I said, 'No way.' They'd have driven her right up the wall."

"You were right," Val told her sister. "Little Leo's much better, too. Dad says he's got a bacterial infection, just like he thought. It's not really serious — or it wouldn't be if Little Leo wasn't so rundown. We're giving him his medicine every four hours, and he really likes that special formula Dad made up. In about a week he ought to be able to start eating meat again. And when he's a little stronger, we're going to give him a bath. He still smells to high heaven."

"Gigi's kind of stinky, too," Erin said, "but I pretend I don't notice. Can we give her a bath, too, one of these days? *Soon?*"

"Not until she's completely over her cold and until Dad says it's okay." Val said. She looked at her watch. "Hey, it's time for Gigi's medicine and some more food. Come on — let's take her down to the kitchen. Maybe Mrs. Racer will let me give it to her for a change."

After supper, Erin put the dirty dishes in the dishwasher and cleaned up the kitchen while Teddy fed Cleveland and the dogs. Then he went out back with Val to take care of the rest of the animals. Val's four rabbits, Flopsy, Mopsy, Cottontail, and Sam, shared a hutch next to the garage. Archibald, the duck, had lived there, too, until Mr. Gebhart had given the Taylors some baby chicks in partial payment for Doc's veterinary services. Teddy had immediately claimed the chicks as his very own, and with Doc's help had constructed a sturdy chicken coop next to the hutch. Now Archibald had moved in with the chicks, and not a moment too soon, Val thought. Archie was beginning to think he was a rabbit and followed Flopsy around as though she were his mother. Val wouldn't have been at all surprised if he'd started hopping and eating carrots.

While Teddy fed his feathered friends, Val gave

the rabbits their dinner. She snuggled each one and apologized for neglecting them lately, leaving them lots of lettuce and celery as a peace offering. Then she hurried back to the house. Even though the essay for the Humane Society contest wasn't due for a week, she wanted to get started on it right away.

"Sorry, Cleveland — I'm afraid you can't come in," Val said as the big orange cat tried to slip past her into her room. "Gigi's not up to seeing visitors yet. She needs lots of rest and quiet."

She closed the door firmly, leaving an indignant Cleveland sitting out in the hall. Gigi was curled up in her box. As soon as she saw Val, she leaped out and scurried over, scrambling up Val's leg and chattering a mile a minute. Val patted her, then put her back into the carton.

"Rest and quiet," she repeated. "I'm glad you're feeling better, but you're not completely well, not by a long shot. Now you stay put — I have homework to do."

Val sat down at her desk and pulled a notebook out from under a pile of textbooks. She chewed the end of her pencil, thinking hard. What should she choose as her topic? As Mr. Steele had said, she felt very strongly about the responsibility of humans for the welfare of animals. Maybe she should write about how hard it was to enforce the laws that were supposed to protect animals. Or what about experiments on laboratory animals? Or maybe she should concentrate on menageries like Mr. Zefferelli's where the animals were undernourished and forced to live in filth? Or how about. . . .

It took most of an hour for Val to come to a decision. She would write about a problem that was very close to her heart — people who abandon their pets when they decide they don't want them anymore. Bright, bouncy little Jocko had joined the Taylor family in just that way. Val had found him tied to a parking meter on the main street of Essex a year and a half ago. The puppy was wearing a collar but no tags so there was no way of tracing his owner. Val had kept coming back time and time again, hoping that someone would claim him, but nobody did. So she had put the little dog in the basket of her bike and brought him home. They put lost-and-found ads in the local paper, but no one ever called.

Jocko's story had a happy ending, but many others didn't. The Humane Society shelter was full of strays and abandoned pets waiting to be adopted. It made Val's blood boil to know that otherwise decent people could be so cruel and heartless as to dump an animal the way you'd toss out a bag of garbage. Yes, that would be the subject of her essay.

She began to write.

Have you ever wondered where all the stray dogs and cats come from that end up in animal shel-

ters? Have you ever fed a homeless animal, then sent it on its way. . . .

Val scribbled away until her cramped fingers warned her it was time to stop and attend to her other homework. Before she began to read her history assignment, she glanced down at Gigi. The little monkey was sound asleep. Gigi and Little Leo had been abandoned, too, but they were among the lucky ones. Val wished she could provide a home for every unwanted, unloved animal in the world. Since she knew that was impossible, she was happy that she and her family could save at least a few of them.

Smiling, Val picked up her history book. Three chapters, then bath and bed. She yawned and stretched. It had been a busy two days, and the rest of the week promised to be every bit as hectic. Tomorrow, though, Val promised herself, she'd sneak off with The Ghost for a ride if things were quiet at Animal Inn.

"Vallie?" It was Teddy, standing in the doorway of her room. He was wearing his pajamas and holding Fuzzy-Wuzzy, the teddy bear that first Val, then Erin, and now Teddy had loved almost to death. Teddy hid Fuzzy-Wuzzy in the closet when his friends came over to play, but every night he slept with the bear in his arms.

"Aren't you going to tuck me in?" Teddy asked.

"I already said good-night to Dad, and I've been waiting for you."

Val put down her book and got up, feeling guilty. She'd been so wrapped up in her essay and in her own thoughts that she'd forgotten the nightly ritual. As rough-and-tumble as he seemed on the outside, Teddy was still a little boy who missed his mother very much and needed all the love he could get.

"Sure, I am," she said, tousling his golden-brown curls. "And I'll tuck Fuzzy-Wuzzy in, too."

"You won't ever tell Eric and Billy that I still sleep with him, will you?" Teddy asked anxiously as he hopped into bed.

"Never. Cross my heart and hope to die," said Val. "Good night, sleep tight. . . ."

". . . don't let the bedbugs bite," Teddy finished. " 'Night, Val."

Val tucked the covers in tight all around. " 'Night, Teddy," she said.

Chapter 6

By the beginning of the following week, both Little Leo and Gigi were much better. On Tuesday, Doc decided that Little Leo was well enough to be taken out of his cage in intensive care. The problem was where to put him until a permanent home could be found.

Val suggested that the lion cub might move into the barn of the Large Animal Clinic, where The Gray Ghost had his stall. So Toby prepared a space, and Little Leo was brought into the barn. But the minute Toby and Val entered with him, the other animals began to fret and snort. Mr. Eberhart's cow, Daisy, who was recovering from surgery, started tossing her head and mooing, pacing around her stall so frantically that Val was afraid she'd rip out her stitches. Patches Gerber, a large hog with arthritis, limped around in circles, grunting and squealing. Even The Ghost, who was usually a calm, placid animal, became upset. He danced back and forth, laid back his ears, and nickered, lashing out with his hooves and striking the walls of his box stall.

"What's the matter with them, anyway?" Toby asked, puzzled.

"You got me," Val said. "It's as if they were scared to death."

"What's to be scared of? Little Leo's only a baby lion," Toby said.

Suddenly light dawned. "That's it!" Val cried. "Boy, are we dumb! We should have known."

"Known what?"

"Little Leo may be only a cub, but he's still a lion," Val told him. "The other animals must have picked up his scent. They don't know he's just a baby. All they know is 'lion,' and they're scared to death."

"Come on, Val," Toby scoffed. "What do farm animals know from lions? They've never smelled a lion in their lives."

"Maybe not, but somehow they *know*," Val insisted. "I guess it's like the way birds know how to make nests even though nobody ever taught them. It has to be instinct. We can't keep Little Leo in here. It'll drive the other animals crazy."

Thump! One of The Ghost's hooves made sharp contact with a wall. Daisy Eberhart mooed and charged the door of her stall, horns lowered. Patches Gerber let out an ear-piercing squeal.

"It's almost like they know that Leo's started eating raw meat again, and they're afraid his next meal will be them!" Val said.

Little Leo, securely held in Toby's arms, began making growling noises in his throat and lashing his tail, the way Cleveland did when he saw a bird that looked like lunch.

"So where do we put him?" Toby asked, holding the lion cub more tightly. *"Ouch!"* he yelled, as Leo's claws sank into his shoulder. "Cut that out, Leo! I'm your pal, remember?"

Val made a quick decision. "We'll put him in the toolshed for now," she said. "We'll make him a nice cozy bed in the corner, and he'll be downwind of the other animals. But he can't stay there forever. Oh, dear! How are we ever going to find a home for him?"

"What about Wildlife Farm?" Toby asked as he followed her to the toolshed. Toby was talking about a place that had just opened outside of Lancaster where they had a petting zoo. "I bet they'd be glad to take him as soon as he's completely well. They take real good care of their animals. It's nothing like Mr. Zefferelli's menagerie."

"That's a thought. I'd forgotten about Wildlife Farm. Maybe they'd take Gigi, too," said Val. She opened the door of the toolshed and peered inside. Mike kept everything very neat and clean — all the tools and equipment for the maintenance of Animal Inn were in their proper places, well-oiled and in excellent condition. There was even a stack of carefully folded burlap feed sacks in one corner that would make a perfect bed for a small lion cub.

"Okay, Little Leo," she said. "Welcome to your new home." She giggled. "Guess we better warn Mike tonight that we've turned his toolshed into a lion's den. He might be kind of surprised to open the door and find Little Leo snuggled up next to the lawn mower!"

The lion cub jumped out of Toby's arms and began wandering around, sniffing at everything. As Toby and Val watched, he went over to the pile of sacks and, after pawing at them once or twice, hopped on top of the pile. He turned around three times, then settled down with a contented sigh, burying his nose between his oversized paws.

"He likes it," Toby said. "I'll make a sign to put on the door: DANGER — SLEEPING LION."

Val cocked her head, listening. "Everybody seems to have calmed down. That's good. Come on, Toby. Dad's probably wondering where we are."

Back at the Taylors' house, Gigi also was recovering rapidly. The little monkey was no longer content to spend her days in the carton in Val's room, or in Erin's doll bed. As her health returned, she became more and more adventurous. Val would come home from school or from her job at Animal Inn to find that Gigi had spent the day very busily indeed. Val discovered all her shoes scattered across the room one day when she'd forgotten to close her closet door. And another day, Gigi had managed to pry open one of her bureau drawers and had taken out all Val's socks and underwear, strewing them here and there.

Val began to get a little annoyed when on Thursday she found her biology notes removed from her notebook and the pages thrown all over the floor. Gigi was scampering around the room, one of Erin's pink satin ballet slippers perched on her head like an outlandish cap, the other slipper clutched in her little paws.

"Gigi! Where did you get those?" Val cried, trying without success to get hold of the slippers.

"It's okay, Vallie," Erin said cheerfully, coming into her room. "I was giving Gigi a ballet lesson after school, and I guess she decided that the slippers were hers. Isn't she just the cutest thing?"

"I guess," Val said, gathering up the pages of her biology notebook. "But I'm not exactly thrilled with her tearing up my notes."

"Oh, well, she's just a little monkey. What do you expect?" Erin said. "I gave her a bath today, too. She *loved* it. Smell her! I used your herbal shampoo and the aloe rinse. She smells just like flowers."

Val sniffed. "Yes, I guess she does."

"You know, Vallie, I bet Gigi could learn to be a ballet dancer. She has real talent," Erin said. "I asked Mrs. Racer if she'd make her a little tutu like the one she made me, and Mrs. Racer said she would. Gigi will look so cute!"

"Great," Val said. "She won't be the first monkey biology student, that's for sure. Erin, why don't you keep her in your room for a while? I have to type my essay for the Humane Society contest — it's due tomorrow, and the one thing I don't need is Gigi's help. She's fascinated by the typewriter. If she's here while I work, she'll probably insist on helping me, and that kind of help I don't need."

"Gee, Vallie, I thought you were such an animal lover," Erin said sadly.

"I am," Val told her. "But this essay is really important to me, and it's important for The Ghost. I need to win the prize money so I can save up for the operation The Ghost needs on his eyes. You know that, Erin. I can't concentrate with Gigi chattering and running around my room."

But she gave the monkey a quick cuddle and hug (Gigi *did* smell like flowers and herbs, Val noticed), then handed her over to Erin.

"I'll bring her back in time for bed," Erin promised. "Gigi, let's go take a look at some of my favorite ballet books. I bet, with practice, you could learn how to dance like a real ballerina!"

Val settled herself at her desk and began to type from the handwritten draft she'd been working on for days. Cleveland, after checking to see that the monkey was nowhere in sight, sidled into the room and took up his customary place on the desk, his large furry body covering most of Val's notes. But Val didn't mind. Anytime she couldn't read what she'd written, all she had to do was heft a section of Cleveland and peer underneath. She was used to working this way. With the background music of Cleveland's contented purr, she finished her typing. She was happy to be finished at last, and as she tore the handwritten copy into little pieces she thought again about how nice it would be to win the contest. She dropped the pieces of paper into the wastebasket.

By now it was almost ten o'clock, and Val stacked the three and a half pages neatly by the typewriter. It was a good essay, she knew, probably the best she had ever done. She'd win the prize, she was sure of it. Erin had brought Gigi back an hour ago, and the little monkey was curled up peacefully in her bed. Val patted her on the head, then got ready for bed. In the morning, she'd hand in the essay. And no matter how much Lila Bascombe bragged, Val was sure Lila's essay was no better than hers.

* * *

When Val awoke the next morning, she blinked her eyes, unable to believe what she was seeing. It looked like there had been a snowstorm in her room — only it was much too early for snow. And anyway, how could the snow have gotten into her room?

Groggily, Val got out of bed. If it was snow, it wasn't cold. It felt like paper — lots of tiny shreds of paper. She bent down and picked up a handful.

It was paper, all right — it was her essay, turned into confetti!

"Gigi!" she squawked.

From the curtain rod over Val's window, the little monkey beamed down at her and chattered happily.

"Gigi, you *didn't*!" Val wailed.

Gigi hung upside down, looking at Val out of big, mischievous brown eyes.

"Gigi, you *did*!" Val moaned.

Grinning, Gigi swung from the curtain rod to the top of the bureau, then scampered to Val's desk, where she picked up a pencil and stuck it behind one ear.

"I love animals. I love animals. *I love animals,*" Val repeated to herself as she plunked herself down at the typewriter, pulling out a fresh piece of paper. "But I cannot believe I have to write this whole essay over again! I will *not* kill this monkey. She's just playful and mischievous, that's all. I'll retype my essay from memory. I practically know it by heart. I will *not* wring her mangy little neck!"

But it was a very great temptation.

By the time Val had finished retyping all three and a half pages, it was half past eight. She had never been late for school in her entire life, but today she knew she would be. She threw on a shirt and a pair of jeans, stuffed her essay into her bookbag, tucked Gigi under one arm, and dashed into the kitchen. Mrs. Racer was already there and greeted the monkey with open arms.

"Keep a close eye on her, Mrs. Racer," Val said grimly, grabbing a container of yogurt out of the refrigerator and stuffing an apple in her pocket. "And keep her out of my room if you can."

Mrs. Racer's eyes widened. "I thought she was supposed to stay in your room," she said.

"That was before she tore up my essay!" Val muttered. "Gotta run. See you later!"

Mrs. Racer stared after her as Val bolted out the door and leaped onto her bike. Gigi wrapped her arms around the housekeeper's neck and chattered cheerfully.

Pedaling furiously toward Hamilton, Val was still seething. She kept telling herself that it wasn't really Gigi's fault. How could the monkey know that those pieces of paper were so important to Val? She couldn't, of course. But the fact of the matter was, Gigi was getting spoiled. Nobody ever punished her when she did something mischievous, like ripping up Val's biology notes.

"I guess I should have spanked her or something," Val thought. But Gigi was so cute and funny, and she'd been so sick and miserable that nobody had the heart to discipline her. Erin hadn't even minded when Gigi had taken her precious toe shoes, and Teddy had just laughed when the monkey had snatched his beloved Phillies baseball cap right off his head and scampered away with it to the top of the china cabinet in the dining room. Mrs. Racer was just as bad — she treated Gigi like a naughty but adorable child.

"We've got to find a home for her and Little Leo, and *soon*," Val decided. The longer the monkey stayed with the Taylors, the more attached to her the rest of the family would become. It was kind of funny, when you thought about it. Usually it was Val who championed any animal that came along, but now she was looking forward to the day when she could call her room her own again. Cleveland would be glad to see the last of Gigi, too, Val knew. If an orange cat could be green with envy, Cleveland would be. Every day when Val came home, she found Cleveland sitting outside the door of her room, glaring at her. Cleveland felt he'd been replaced by the monkey, and no matter how often Val picked him up and cuddled him and told him Gigi was only a temporary guest, Cleveland just struggled out of her arms and refused to purr.

It didn't help that Gigi was fascinated by Cleveland's tail. Whenever the monkey was permitted to roam the house, she followed Cleveland around, making swipes at the cat's angrily switching tail. Cleveland would try to attack, but Gigi was much too quick, so Cleveland had learned to hide under the couch, tail wrapped around himself, when Gigi came in sight.

Val leaped off her bike, flung it into the bike rack, and dashed up the steps to Hamilton's front door. She burst into the English classroom just as Lila Bascombe was collecting the last essay. Val pulled hers out of her knapsack and thrust it at Lila, then collapsed into her seat.

"What happened?" Jill whispered. "I thought maybe you were sick or something when you didn't show up in homeroom."

"Monkey business!" Val whispered back. "I'll tell you about it later." She glanced around the room, noticing for the first time that the teacher wasn't there. "Where's Mr. Steele?" she asked.

"He's not in today. We have a substitute, but she stepped out for a minute," Jill told her.

Just then a small, thin woman wearing horn-rimmed glasses bustled into the room. "Sorry, class. I had to speak to the principal," she said. "Have you collected all the essays, Lily?"

"That's *Lila*," Lila corrected with a frown. "And yes, I did. They're on the desk."

"Very good. Now let's turn to page seventy-three in our anthology of American poetry. Today we are going to discuss Joyce Kilmer's wonderful poem, 'Trees.' "

"Yuck!" Jill groaned under her breath. "How boring!"

Val giggled. "What can you expect from a man whose first name is Joyce?" she whispered, and Jill giggled, too.

"Girls! You two in the back — perhaps you'd like to share the joke," the teacher snapped.

"No, ma'am," Jill said sweetly. "On second thought, it wasn't really all that funny."

Lila's hand shot up. "May I read the poem aloud, Ms. Bradley?" she asked. "I just *love* nature poetry."

Val and Jill glanced at each other and mouthed silently, "Yuck!"

At Ms. Bradley's nod, Lila stood up, smoothed her hair with one hand, and began to read in a loud sing-song, " 'I think that I shall never see/A poem lovely as a tree. . . .' "

Jill leaned over and scrawled in Val's notebook,

I wish I didn't have to hear
The voice of Lila in my ear.

Val grinned and wrote,

'Cause when I do, I want to flee,
Or chase her up that stupid tree!

Stifling more giggles, the girls sat back to endure the rest of Lila's recitation.

Chapter 7

Val wasn't officially on duty at Animal Inn that afternoon, but though Jill asked her to go to the East Side Mall with her after school, Val said no. What she really wanted to do was spend some time with The Ghost, and that was much more important than buying new sneakers. Besides, Val was sure that the *old* sneakers that Gigi had hidden the other day would turn up some time. At least, she hoped so.

"I don't know, Ghost." Val sighed as she saddled the big gray horse. "I love animals, I really do. Only Gigi drives me crazy! I'd *love* to love her, but I just can't."

The Ghost nodded his head, as though he was agreeing with her. Then he snorted and pawed the ground, eager to be off for their long-awaited ride.

Val grinned and grasped his reins. "I know just how you feel," she told him. "What we need is fresh air, sunshine, and exercise."

A moment later, Val was on The Ghost's back and they were heading for the open countryside that stretched behind Animal Inn. Val wished she could let The Ghost have a good gallop, but until his cataracts were removed, she knew she had to hold him to a sedate trot. Even if she'd saved up enough money, Doc had told her that they would have to wait until the cataracts had reached a certain stage before surgery could take place.

"But don't worry, Ghost," Val said, patting his satiny neck. "When the time comes, you'll have that operation, I promise. And if I win the essay contest, that's fifty dollars more to put in the bank."

Val felt a surge of love for her horse, and pride in his beauty and strength. They rode in silence for a while. Finally she said, "I guess there's nothing I can do about it — about how I feel about Gigi, I mean," she added, so The Ghost wouldn't be confused. "It's like people. You love some people, and you like some people, and then there are some who just plain rub you the wrong way — like Lila Bascombe. And I won't have to put up with Gigi much longer because she's well enough to go to Wildlife Farm." Suddenly she giggled. "I wish there were a People Farm! I'd ship Lila there so fast it'd make her head swim!"

Val and Jill had agreed to meet at the Taylors' after Jill had finished her shopping and Val had had her ride. As Val biked to a stop in front of the house, she saw Jill coming down the street carrying a shopping bag. Apparently her friend had found what she was looking for — and probably several other things as well, if Val knew Jill.

The girls went inside, and Jocko and Sunshine greeted them with their usual barks and leaps of joy.

"Where's Cleveland?" Jill asked, patting first one dog, then the other.

"Probably sulking upstairs in front of my door," Val said. "He's mad at me because Gigi's been living in my room. I'll go get him."

She went upstairs, but there was no big orange cat glowering at her in the hall. Oh, well, Val thought, he's probably hiding out somewhere — maybe under the sofa.

She came downstairs and crouched on hands and knees in front of the sofa, peering underneath.

"Cleveland?" she called. "Cleveland, are you in there?"

No response, and no sign of the cat.

"That you, Vallie?" Mrs. Racer came into the room, wiping her hands on her apron. "Oh, hello, Jill."

"Hi, Mrs. Racer," Jill said.

"Jill's eating over, Mrs. Racer," Val said. "That won't be any problem, will it?"

"No sir, not one bit. I made a nice beef stew — there's plenty. Macaroni and cheese for you, Val."

"Did Gigi behave herself today?" Val asked.

"Well. . . ." Mrs. Racer looked a little uncomfortable. "She *did* get into a little trouble. But it wasn't her fault," she added quickly. "Poor little thing! She hadn't ought to do that to Cleveland, but then Cleveland hadn't ought to go for her like he did."

Val narrowed her eyes. "Mrs. Racer, where *is* Cleveland? And what happened?"

"Oh, dear," Mrs. Racer sighed. "Tell you the truth, Vallie, I don't know where Cleveland is. He lit out of here so fast I couldn't see where he was headed. Guess he didn't realize that Gigi was only playing when she took a bite out of his tail. . . ."

"A bite out of his *tail*!" Val squawked. "Oh, poor Cleveland!"

"Not a *big* bite," Mrs. Racer said. "Just more like a little nip. Only I guess Cleveland was kind of mad because Gigi broke his food dish. . . ."

"Gigi broke Cleveland's bowl? The one I made in ceramics class?"

"She didn't mean to. She was just teasing. She picked it up, and I guess she didn't know how heavy it was — she's such a little bit of a thing — and she dropped it on the floor. It's going to be all right, Vallie. It only broke in two pieces, and Teddy glued them back together. Cleveland took off after Gigi, but Gigi jumped onto the dining room table and then Cleveland followed her. That's when he knocked over the vase of flowers. You never saw such a mess! But I cleaned it up, and then. . . ."

"Mrs. Racer, *when did Gigi bite Cleveland's tail?*" Val shouted.

"That was later, after Gigi chased him under the sofa. Cleveland's tail was sticking out, so Gigi. . . ."

"Bit it," Val finished. "Mrs. Racer, I am going to *murder* that monkey!"

"Now, Vallie, don't get all upset," Mrs. Racer said. "I paddled her little bottom gentle-like, and I put her in the pantry. She's there now. You should have seen her little face. She looked so sad!"

"Good!" Val cried. "C'mon, Jill. We have to find Cleveland. That poor cat has a monkey-bite on his tail, and I bet he thinks nobody loves him.

" 'Bye, Mrs. Racer," Jill called as Val grabbed her hand and dragged her out of the house. "I'm sure the beef stew will be delicious!"

Val paused in the middle of the path leading to the front door. "If I were Cleveland and a nasty monkey had taken a bite out of my tail, where would I go?" she asked aloud.

"Maybe up a tree?" Jill suggested.

"Maybe," Val agreed. "But there are an awful lot of trees in this neighborhood. Guess we better start calling. Jill, you go down the block and I'll go up. We'll both call him — only you have to know how."

"Come on, Val. What's so hard about calling a cat?" Jill asked. "I'll just call his name — 'Here, Cleveland.' Right?"

"Wrong," Val said. "You have to call kind of high, and you say, 'Here, kitty, kitty, kitty. Here, puss, puss, puss.' "

"You've got to be kidding!" said Jill. "I'll feel like an idiot."

"Jill, trust me. Just do what I say, okay?"

Jill rolled her eyes. "Okay. But I bet we get every cat in the neighborhood."

"I don't care if we get every cat in the neighborhood," Val said. "The main thing is, we get Cleveland. Start calling."

So Jill started off down the block, calling at the top of her lungs, and Val started in the opposite direction.

Half an hour later, they met in front of the Taylors' house. No Cleveland.

"What do we do now?" Jill asked.

"I don't know," Val said with a sigh. Then suddenly she had an idea. "Teddy's tree house! Maybe Cleveland's there. Let's look."

The girls hurried around to the backyard, and clambered up the ladder that led to the tree house. Val led the way, and when her head cleared the tree house floor, she saw a large orange shape huddled in one corner.

"Here he is!" she called over her shoulder.

Jill scrambled up after her, to find Val sitting cross-legged on the floor, with Cleveland in her arms.

"It didn't break the skin," Val told her happily. "Cleveland has such thick fur that I guess Gigi's teeth couldn't get through it. There, there, Cleveland. It's all right. Everybody loves you — everybody except Gigi, that is. And she's going to be leaving very soon, honest."

Cleveland allowed himself to be stroked and snuggled, but he didn't purr. Every now and then he turned around to check out his injured tail. Finally, after Val and Jill had petted and soothed him and told him that he was the most wonderful cat in the world, he began to relax, and a very small, very weak purr burbled up in his throat.

"That's more like it," Val said, scratching him under his chin. "Come on, Cleveland. I'll give you a can of tuna for dinner. And I promise Gigi won't get within a mile of it!"

"Dad, we have to get rid of Gigi," Val announced that night as she, Doc, Teddy, Erin, and Jill sat around the butcher block table in the kitchen, eating the good supper that Mrs. Racer had prepared. "She's driving Cleveland and me crazy. And she's well enough, so she can go to Wildlife Farm with Little Leo."

"Oh, no, Daddy!" Erin cried. "Gigi's adorable. She's the best pet we ever had. She lets me dress her up in Elizabeth's clothes, and Mrs. Racer is making a tutu for her just like mine. I was going to ask Miss Tamara if I can do a dance with Gigi at the next recital."

"*If* you have any toe shoes left," Val said. "Didn't I hear you telling Mrs. Racer that Gigi tore the ribbons off your best slippers?"

"Well, yes, I guess she did. But that's okay — Mrs. Racer sewed them back on," Erin told her. She turned to her father. "Daddy, can't we let Gigi out of the pantry now? I'm sure she's learned her lesson, and she'll never bite Cleveland's tail again."

"You bet she won't!" Val snapped. "Remember when you got mad at Teddy's ferret and told him we were going to have fried ferret for dinner? Well, if Gigi lays a paw or a tooth on Cleveland again, the main course on the menu will be monkey stew!"

"Oh, Vallie! That's gross!" Erin wailed.

"Yeah, Vallie. How come you're so mean about Gigi?" Teddy asked.

"Vallie's not being mean, Teddy. She's being realistic," Doc said. "The original idea was to keep Gigi here until she got well enough to move on to another home. She's well enough now, and so is Little Leo. He doesn't like living in the toolshed, but there's nowhere else to put him at Animal Inn. We'll take them both to Wildlife Farm this weekend. I've already called and spoken to the owners. They're eager to add a monkey and a lion cub to their collection. And I've been in touch with the Humane Society in Lancaster. They tell me that Wildlife Farm is clean and well-run. The staff really care about the animals. I'm sure Gigi and Leo will be very happy there, and it will be better for them than being cooped up with us."

"But *we* won't be happy," Teddy muttered. "Except mean old Vallie. *She'll* be happy, all right!"

"Teddy, that's enough," Doc said sternly. "The subject is closed. And now I guess you might as well let Gigi out of the pantry, Erin."

Erin leaped up and ran to open the pantry door.

"Oh, no!" she cried. "Oh, Gigi, what have you done?"

"What *has* she done?" Jill asked.

Everyone crowded around the door to see. Gigi was perched on the shelf below the pantry cupboard. She looked like a monkey ghost, covered from head to tail tip with white. The entire pantry floor was covered in drifts of white as well. Just like my room this morning, Val thought. Only this time the "snow" was flour.

"It's all my fault," Erin sighed. "I latched all the cupboard doors like Mrs. Racer said, but I forgot to put away the flour canister."

"Looks like it's time to give Gigi another bath," Val said wearily. "If there's any shampoo left, that is."

"Boy, Gigi, you really did it this time!" Teddy said admiringly. "That's about the biggest mess I ever saw."

"It is indeed," Doc said. "And since you and Erin have turned into Gigi's champions, the two of you may have the privilege of cleaning it up."

Teddy's face fell. "But we didn't do it, Gigi did!"

"True," Doc agreed. "But since she's just a poor little animal who doesn't know any better and can't clean up after herself, you'll have to do it for her."

"That's not fair," Erin grumbled.

"It wasn't fair that Gigi tore up my essay, either," Val pointed out. "And it wasn't fair that I had to type the whole thing all over so I was late for school for the very first time ever. Come on, Jill. We'll clean up the monkey while Teddy and Erin clean up the mess."

"Wow! This is going to be fun," Jill said, grinning. "It's like I keep saying — you never know what's going to happen next at your house!"

"Val, would you stay after class for a minute?" Mr. Steele asked two days later at the end of English period.

"Yes, sir," Val said. She wondered what he

wanted to speak to her about. Maybe he'd read her essay and wanted to tell her he thought it was good. Or maybe he'd read her essay and thought it was terrible. Or maybe he didn't want to talk about her essay at all.

"I'll wait for you outside," Jill said on her way to the classroom door. Val nodded and went up to Mr. Steele's desk.

"You know, Val, I never thought I'd have to say this," he began, "but I'm disappointed in you."

Val stared at him and felt her face flaming. He *had* read her essay, and he *did* hate it! She wanted to sink through the floor.

"I — I'm sorry, Mr. Steele. I guess I left some things out. But that's because the monkey tore it up. . . ."

Mr. Steele shook his head sadly. "I've heard some lame excuses for not handing in work, but this one takes the cake. I'm really surprised at you, Val. You're one of my best students, and this topic is right up your alley. I would have understood if you told me the real reason you didn't do the assignment, but I'm afraid I can't buy a story about a monkey tearing up your essay."

"But I *did* do the assignment! I did it *twice*!" Val cried. "And the monkey *did* tear up the first one I did — we're taking care of this monkey because she's been sick, only she's lots better now — and I'd torn up my first draft and thrown it away so I had to start all over from scratch, which was why I was late for school the day before yesterday, only you weren't here so you didn't know, and — "

"Hold it! Slow down. I think I lost the thread somewhere," Mr. Steele said. "Let me see if I've got it straight so far. You wrote the essay, but the monkey tore it up, so you did it over, right?"

"That's right," Val said eagerly. "And I handed it in to Lila. She was collecting them for Ms. Bradley, the substitute. Mine was the last one. Ask my friend Jill if you don't believe me."

Mr. Steele smiled. "I do believe you, Val, and I'm sorry I spoke to you so harshly. But the fact remains that when I went over the essays before handing them over to the Humane Society, there was nothing there with your name on it."

Val narrowed her eyes. She was beginning to smell a rat, and the name of the rat was Lila Bascombe.

"Mr. Steele," she said grimly, "I gave my essay to Lila. I really did."

"Then it must have gotten misplaced somehow," Mr. Steele said with a sigh. "I'll check with Ms. Bradley — I believe she's in the building, covering for somebody else. It's possible that your essay might have been mixed up with some of her papers.

I'm really sorry, Val. I have to admit I assumed you'd win the contest hands down."

"Thanks, Mr. Steele," Val said, forcing a smile. "But that won't happen now."

"Val? You coming?" Jill asked, poking her head in the door. "Sorry, Mr. Steele, but we'll be late for history if we don't get moving."

"I understand," Mr. Steele said. "See you tomorrow in class."

Val nodded, the smile still pasted on her face, and hurried to join Jill.

"What was that all about?" Jill asked.

"My essay. It's lost," Val said.

"Lost? But that's crazy. I saw you hand it in to. . . ."

"Lila Bascombe," Val finished.

"Lila Bascombe," Jill echoed.

The girls looked at each other.

" 'Lost' my eye!" Jill exploded. "I bet Lila very conveniently managed to 'lose' it in the wastebasket!"

"I wouldn't be one bit surprised," Val said. "She's just dying to get even with me, and this is a great way to do it."

"We'll tackle her at lunch," Jill said. "And we'll get the truth out of her if we have to tie her to her chair!"

Chapter 8

But finding Lila wasn't all that easy. She seemed to have disappeared off the face of the earth — or at least off the face of Hamilton Junior High. As soon as history class was over, Val and Jill headed for the gym. Lila was in their gym class, and they expected to corner her in the locker room. Lila, however, wasn't there. When Val asked Courtney, one of Lila's friends, where she was, Courtney told her icily that Lila had a stomachache and had been excused from gym. She'd gone to the nurse's office to lie down.

"Ow!" Jill cried, clapping a hand to her forehead.

"What's the matter, Jill?" Val asked anxiously. "Are you all right?"

Jill staggered a little, still clutching her head, and leaned against the bank of lockers. "My head — it's *killing* me. My mother had a migraine this morning. I think I caught it."

Courtney raised an eyebrow. "Come off it, Jill.

My mother gets migraines all the time, and I happen to know they're not contagious."

"Oh, yeah?" Jill snapped. "Maybe your mother's migraines are different from *my* mother's migraines. Oh, ow!" she moaned again. "I'd better tell Ms. Bock that I can't take gym today. I'm going straight to the nurse's office."

Val got the message. "Yes, you better do that, Jill. You're looking very pale. And while you're in the nurse's office, you and Lila can have a *nice talk*."

"Where's the door?" Jill mumbled, stretching out her arms in front of her. "I'm seeing purple spots before my eyes. I hope I don't faint. . . ."

Val took Jill's hand. "I'll help you," she said, putting on a worried expression for Courtney's benefit. As soon as they were outside the locker room, she whispered, "Good thinking! Let me know what you find out."

"I sure will. But we have to make this look good, or Ms. Bock won't let me go. She knows how much I hate gym. You kind of hold me up, like I might pass out any minute."

Val put her arm around Jill's shoulders, and the two girls went into the gym. They found Ms. Bock putting up the volleyball net. She looked at Jill suspiciously as Val explained Jill's sudden headache, but she wrote out a pass to the nurse's office.

"Maybe I'd better go with her," Val suggested. "She's feeling pretty bad."

"No, I'll be all right," Jill said with a brave little smile. "I can't tell you how sorry I am to miss volleyball, Ms. Bock," she added.

"I'm sure you are," Ms. Bock said, but her tone was skeptical. "Val, hurry up and change. If you're not too worried about your friend's health to play, that is."

"Oh, no, I'm not worried at all — I mean, I'm not *very* worried," Val told her.

"Ooooh," Jill moaned as she staggered out of the gym.

Ms. Bock looked after her. "I don't know about that girl," she said with a sigh. "Last week it was an ingrown toenail, this week it's a migraine. I wonder what she'll think up next week?"

Val didn't answer, just headed back to the locker room. Though she loved gym as a rule because she was very good at sports, she could hardly wait for class to be over so she could find out what Jill had learned.

"Nothing," Jill said when Val met her outside the nurse's office after gym.

"What do you mean, 'nothing'?" Val asked. "She wouldn't talk, or what?"

"She wasn't there," Jill told her. "I came in,

doing my dying swan routine, and Mrs. Becker gave me some aspirin and made me lie down on one of those miserable cots — they're hard as a rock. But there was nobody else in the room. When Mrs. Becker went out for a few minutes, I checked behind the screen just to make sure, but Lila wasn't hiding there."

"What do you suppose happened to her?" Val asked.

"Her mother came to take her home," Jill said. "I finally asked Mrs. Becker about her. I pretended I was all worried about my *dear* friend Lila and asked where she was. And Mrs. Becker said that Mrs. Bascombe had picked her up. Lila had called her from the office."

"Rats!" said Val. "We can't very well go banging on her door, I guess. That means we'll have to wait till tomorrow."

"And tomorrow'll be too late as far as your essay is concerned," Jill said sadly. "That's when they're going to announce the winner of the contest. Even if we found out that Lila had squirreled your essay away somewhere and could persuade her to turn it in, the judges' decision would have been made. Double rats!"

"If only I'd had the sense to make a carbon," Val sighed. "But I meant to make a photocopy on the school's machine before I turned it in, and then when Gigi tore up my only copy, I was so mad and in such a rush that I didn't even think about it. Triple rats!"

"Speaking of Gigi, what's happening with her and Little Leo?" Jill asked. "Are they going to Wildlife Farm?"

"Yes, this weekend," Val said. "Erin, Teddy, and Mrs. Racer act like it's the end of the world — as though Dad and I were sending them off to a fate worse than death. It's really weird. Usually I'm the one who begs and pleads to keep an animal, but this time, I'm the bad guy." She made a face. "This essay contest has turned into a real mess all around!"

"It sure has," Jill agreed. "Come on, let's have lunch. Drown your sorrows in a bowl of yogurt."

The girls trudged down the hall in the direction of the cafeteria.

"Jill, how are you feeling? Headache all gone?" It was Ms. Bock, on her way to the teachers' dining room.

Jill forced a wan and sickly smile. "Much better, thank you, Ms. Bock."

"I'm so glad to hear it," the gym teacher said cheerfully. "And since you're well on the road to recovery, I suggest that you make up the period you missed by joining the fifth period gym class this afternoon instead of going to study hall. Otherwise, I'm afraid I'm going to have to give you a failing grade this semester."

"Gee, Ms. Bock, I certainly wouldn't want that," Jill said. "I'll be glad to make up the period this afternoon. Volleyball again?"

"No, this time it's basketball," Ms. Bock said, beaming. "See you at two o'clock, okay?"

"Sure — okay," Jill muttered. After Ms. Bock had continued on her way, Jill turned to Val. "Basketball! If there's anything I hate more than volleyball, it's basketball. I'm so short, they'll probably use me for the ball!"

Val couldn't help giggling. "Just wrap your arms around your knees and keep your head down, and remember to bounce back up when they drop you through the hoop!"

"Very funny," Jill said. "Some friend you are! Boy, I wish I could send Lila as my substitute. I'd love to see some of those jocks dribbling her across the floor." Then she began to giggle, too. "Guess I better have a good big lunch. I'm going to need all the energy I can get."

In English class the next day, Val slid into her seat, her face grim. She'd tried to tell herself that winning the essay contest didn't really matter — that the fifty dollars she might have won had never been certain. But every penny she could save toward The Ghost's operation was precious, and now she didn't even stand a chance of adding to her savings.

"Class, it is my pleasure and privilege to introduce to you Mrs. Pollock, chairman of the board of the Essex Humane Society," Mr. Steele said. "Mrs. Pollock has taken time from her busy schedule to come to Hamilton Junior High in order to present the award for the prize-winning essay in the Humane Society's contest. Mrs. Pollock, the floor is yours."

Mrs. Pollock, who had been standing off to the side of Mr. Steele's desk, stepped forward, smiling with large teeth at the students before her.

"Thank you, Mr. Steele. As you and your pupils already know, the Essex Humane Society is most concerned that young people become aware of the problems involved with the care of our animal friends. As we at the Humane Society like to say, 'Every dog, cat, and pony must have its day!' "

Val cringed. She knew that Mrs. Pollock was a good, hard-working woman who really cared about animals, but Mrs. Pollock had a way of putting things that often made her want to slide under the table. Doc felt the same way, Val knew.

"And that's why we are so pleased at the essays that you and the other English classes at Hamilton Junior High have submitted for our consideration," Mrs. Pollock continued. "I am happy to inform you that the winner of the essay contest is seated right here, in this very room!"

She smiled broadly, looking at each student as she spoke.

Val didn't smile back. She knew that Mrs. Pollock was not referring to her.

"Without further ado, I wish to announce the winner." Mrs. Pollock checked her notes, then looked up. "The winner of the Essex Humane Society essay contest is . . . Lila Bascombe."

Val froze in her seat. She glanced over at Jill, who crossed her eyes and stuck out her tongue just long enough for Val to see.

Lila, smiling modestly, stood up, acknowledging the applause of her classmates.

"Thank you, Mrs. Pollock," she said sweetly. "I want you to know how much I appreciate this honor. I've always loved animals. . . ."

(Val and Jill looked at each other again, scowling.)

" . . . and I am delighted that the Humane Society has seen fit to choose my essay as the best out of the entire school."

"Congratulations, Lila," said Mr. Steele.

"Thank you, Mr. Steele," Lila replied, fluttering her lashes.

"Before Mrs. Pollock hands over the check, I think it would be appropriate for Lila to read her winning essay to the class," Mr. Steele said.

Lila looked startled. "Uh . . . well, I don't know . . ." she mumbled.

"Now, now, Lila, don't be modest," Mrs. Pollock urged. "I have a copy right here in my hand, just in case you don't have one with you. I think the entire class should hear it. Go ahead, dear." She thrust the paper at Lila. "Read it."

Lila took the paper and stared at it for a long moment.

"I . . . I really don't think . . ." she began.

"Lila, read it," Mr. Steele commanded.

Lila took a deep breath and glanced over to where Val and Jill were sitting. Then she began to read in a very low monotone, very fast.

"Speak up, dear. We can't hear you," Mrs. Pollock fluted.

Lila squared her shoulders, flipped a strand of glossy dark hair over one shoulder, and started again, this time in a voice loud enough for everyone to hear.

"Have you ever wondered where all the stray dogs and cats come from that end up in animal shelters? Have you ever fed a homeless animal, then sent it on its way to the next handout? Have you ever had a pet you couldn't keep, but didn't know what to do with? Did you ever decide that the best thing to do for that pet was to leave it in some nice neighborhood where kind people would be sure to take it in and care for it? If you have, then you know the answer to my first question. The animals that are crowding shelters all over the country have in many cases been abandoned by their owners who no longer want the responsibility of taking care of them. . . ."

Val's jaw dropped as she listened to the familiar words, and her face flushed with astonishment and rage.

Jill looked over at her. "What's the matter, Val?" she whispered. "You look like you're having an attack."

"That essay — Lila's essay . . ." Val stammered.

"Sounds pretty good so far," Jill whispered. "I'm really surprised. I didn't think Lila had it in her."

"She doesn't!" Val hissed. "Jill, that's *my* essay! Word for word! She's reading *my essay*!"

"You're kidding!" Jill gasped. "Are you sure?"

"You bet I'm sure," Val said angrily. "I wrote the whole thing in longhand, and then I typed it twice. I know every single word! Lila didn't 'lose' my essay — she stole it!"

Mr. Steele frowned at Val and Jill, shaking his head slightly. Val, her face still flaming, bit her lip and scrunched down in her seat. Her thoughts were churning. What should she do? Jump up and accuse Lila of stealing her essay in front of the entire class and Mrs. Pollock? No, that wouldn't do any good. Lila would just give one of her sickly-sweet smiles and say that Val was lying. There was no way she could prove she was telling the truth. No one, not even Jill, had read Val's essay, so no one would be able to stand up for her. But it wasn't fair! Lila had won first prize with Val's essay. How could she be such a rotten little sneak?

Jill paid no attention to Mr. Steele. She whispered in Val's ear, "You're not going to let her get away with it, are you? Stand up and tell them what happened!"

Val just shook her head.

"Well, if you won't, I will," Jill said, and raised her hand. But Val grabbed her wrist and yanked it down.

"No, you won't," she whispered. "I don't want to make a scene. I'll talk to Mr. Steele right after class."

"Sure — right after Lila walks off with the prize money that should have been yours," Jill muttered.

"I don't care about the money," Val replied. "Or not much, anyway — but Lila's not going to get away with stealing my essay, nosirree!"

Lila had finished reading, and the class broke into spontaneous applause.

"That was an excellent essay, Lila," Mr. Steele said, shaking her hand.

"It certainly was," Mrs. Pollock added. "All the essays were good, of course, and I wish I could give a prize to every single one of you. But there's only one first prize, and it gives me great pleasure to present this check for fifty dollars to Lila Bascombe on behalf of the Humane Society of Essex, Pennsylvania."

There was more applause as Lila, eyes modestly downcast, accepted the check. Then she turned to Mr. Steele and said, "I want to thank my wonderful English teacher. Without his constant inspiration and support, I never could have written a prize-winning essay, even on a topic so close to my heart as the welfare of our animal friends."

"I think I'm going to throw up," Jill said under her breath. "You'd think she was accepting an Academy Award or something."

"She deserves one," Val mumbled. "That was quite a performance."

Mrs. Pollock went on to present checks for twenty-five and ten dollars to the second and third prize winners. Then Mr. Steele dismissed the class.

"Now!" Jill said, poking Val in the arm. "You tackle Mr. Steele. I'll make sure that Lila doesn't cut out."

Val's heart was pounding so hard she thought it might jump out of her chest. She was tempted to just slink away and lick her wounds in private, but she wouldn't — she couldn't — let Lila walk off with the prize that was rightfully hers. She marched up to the teacher's desk and stood there, her fists clenched at her sides. She was glad that Mrs. Pollock had hurried off. She didn't want to have to explain the whole situation to Mrs. Pollock as well.

"Yes, Val? What is it?" Mr. Steele asked.

"Mr. Steele. . . ." Val swallowed hard, then continued. "Mr. Steele, that essay Lila read. . . ."

"It was an excellent essay," Mr. Steele said. "She deserved the prize. But I'm sorry yours never turned up."

"But it *did*!" Val burst out. "It did, and Lila read it!"

Mr. Steele looked at her as though she'd completely lost her marbles. "I'm not sure I understand," he said. "Are you telling me that Lila's essay is actually yours?"

Val nodded hard. "That's exactly what I'm saying. My essay didn't get mixed up with Ms. Bradley's papers, or get lost somewhere along the way. That was *my essay*! Honest, Mr. Steele, it was!"

Mr. Steele was obviously confused, and beginning to be upset. "Val, this is a very serious accusation you're making."

"It sure is!" Lila said angrily.

Jill had cornered Lila and dragged her over to Mr. Steele's desk. Lila was scowling and clutching the check in her hand.

"I never heard of anything so ridiculous!" she

went on, glaring at Val and at Jill. "I didn't think Val Taylor would be so vindictive as to try to steal my prize money from me! Just because she didn't have time to write an essay because she's so *busy* with her job at that tacky Animal Inn. . . ."

Jill, who was still hanging onto Lila's arm, gave her a vicious pinch, and Lila squealed, "Oooo! You're *hurting* me!"

"Good!" Jill snapped. "Now how about telling the truth for once in your life?"

"Girls, take it easy," Mr. Steele said. "Val, suppose you tell me your version of the story. Then it's Lila's turn."

So Val spilled out her story — how she had retyped her essay after Gigi had destroyed it the first time, and how she had handed it to Lila, and how it had mysteriously disappeared, and how she had recognized the words the minute Lila had begun to read it.

"That's nonsense," Lila said calmly. "Here — look at it. I typed it myself on my new electronic typewriter. It's nothing like your dinky old manual typewriter where the 'r' doesn't print right!"

"How do you know the 'r' doesn't print right if you didn't see my essay?" Val shot back.

"Yes, Lila, how do you know that?" Mr. Steele asked.

"Uh . . . well, I've seen other things Val has

typed," Lila said lamely. "This is my essay, all right! If Val has proof, I'll be interested to see it."

Val's heart sank. She had no proof, no proof at all.

Or did she?

"Mr. Steele," she said, "I tore up my first draft, and the monkey tore up the one I typed, so I don't have any *real* proof."

Lila smirked.

"But because I wrote my essay *three times*," Val continued, "I know it word for word, by heart. Will you listen while I recite it to you?"

Lila looked a little pale, and Mr. Steele looked interested. Jill grinned and said, "All *right*!"

"Let's hear it," said Mr. Steele.

Val took a deep breath. "Have you ever wondered where all the stray dogs and cats come from that end up in animal shelters? Have you ever fed a homeless animal, then sent it on its way to the next handout? Have you ever had a pet you couldn't keep, but didn't know what to do with? Did you ever decide. . . ."

"That's enough, Val," said Mr. Steele. "Lila, do you have anything to say for yourself?"

Lila seemed to shrink before Val's very eyes. "She's got a good memory, that's all," she muttered.

Mr. Steele shot her a sharp glance. He'd been

following Val's words on a copy of Lila's essay, and now he looked up at Val.

"Nobody has that good a memory," he said quietly. "Val's not a tape recorder. It's word perfect. There's no way she could have remembered every single word unless she'd written them herself — *three times*."

"Then you do believe me?" Val asked, her eyes sparkling.

Instead of answering Val's question, Mr. Steele looked straight at Lila. "Lila," he said sternly, "I'm giving you one more chance. Who do you believe? Which one of you is telling the truth here?"

There was a pause. Then Lila said quietly, "Val is."

"Lila, I think you owe Val an apology." Mr. Steele said. "I also think you owe her a check for fifty dollars, and I'd appreciate it if you'd hand it over right now. I'll return it to the Humane Society — they can void it and write a new one, made out to the real winner of the essay contest. And that winner is Valentine Taylor."

"Better believe it!" Jill crowed, giving Val a hug.

Lila tossed her head and dropped the check onto Mr. Steele's desk. "Well, I don't need a measly old fifty dollars, anyway."

"I'm sure you don't," said Mr. Steele. "But I

think you'd like to get a passing grade in English, and at this point, you're not going to get it. Trying to pass off another student's work as your own is a very serious offense, Lila. If you don't want to flunk English this semester, I strongly suggest you write a brand new essay — a thousand words on why it's wrong to cheat. And I want to see it on Monday morning, neatly typed on your electronic typewriter. A thousand words, Lila. Monday morning sharp."

Lila gave him a very dirty look. "My father's on the school board, Mr. Steele. He could make life very unpleasant for any teacher who gives me trouble."

Mr. Steele smiled. "I'm sure he could, Lila. But he might not be terribly pleased to learn that his daughter tried to pass off another girl's essay as her own."

"Monday," Lila mumbled, flouncing off. "A thousand words."

Mr. Steele stood up and reached out to shake Val's hand as Lila marched out the door. "Congratulations, Val Taylor. I'll look forward to seeing your essay printed in *The Essex Gazette*. And I'll see that the check is mailed to you first thing tomorrow morning."

Val beamed. "Thanks, Mr. Steele. Thanks an awful lot!"

Chapter 9

"I just can't believe anybody would be such a crook!" Erin said that night after Val had told her family about Lila's attempt to pass off Val's essay as her own. "If Mr. Steele hadn't made her read the essay aloud, you never would have known and Lila would have gotten away with it."

"I'd have known when it was printed in the *Gazette*," Val said. "But by then Lila would have cashed the check and bought that fancy dress, and I wouldn't have had a prayer of adding fifty dollars to The Ghost's operation fund."

"If it was me," Teddy put in, "I'd have punched her out the minute she started reading. Pow! Right in the kisser!"

"No, you would not," Doc said firmly. "Or at least I hope you wouldn't. Vallie handled the situation in exactly the right way, and I'm proud of her." He put one arm around Val and gave her a hug. "Mrs. Pollock called me today after she'd spoken to Mr. Steele. She hadn't understood why you hadn't submitted an entry, Vallie, but she hadn't mentioned it to me before because she knew that I wanted to remain uninvolved in the contest. It would have looked a little strange if the father of one of the contestants had anything to say about selecting the winner. She sends her congratulations, Vallie, and she'll drop the check off at Animal Inn tomorrow morning."

Val sighed happily. "That's wonderful." Then she grinned. "And what's even more wonderful is that Lila's going to spend a miserable weekend grinding out a thousand words on why it's wrong to cheat!"

"Hey, I have a great idea," Teddy said, his eyes sparkling with mischief. "When she's finished, we could send Gigi over to her house, and Gigi could tear up her essay like she did Vallie's. Then Lila'd have to do it all over again!"

Everyone laughed, even Doc.

Rrroow!

Cleveland stalked across the room and leaped up in Val's lap, purring loudly. Val stroked his fur.

"Speaking of Gigi, where is she?" she asked. "You must have put her away somewhere really secure, or Cleveland wouldn't be purring like this."

"She's in the basement," Erin said. "I don't know why we didn't think of putting her there before. I took her down with me while I was doing my ballet exercises after school, the way I usually do, and she was having such fun that I left her there. She loves hanging by her tail from the barre, and making faces at herself in the mirror. I closed the door to the kitchen real tight when I came up, too, so she can't get into any trouble."

"And of course you closed the door into the laundry room," Doc said.

Silence.

Then, "The laundry room?" Erin echoed. "Gee, I'm not sure. . . ."

Val leaped to her feet, dumping an indignant Cleveland on the floor.

"Soap powder!" she cried.

"Fabric softener! Bleach!" Doc groaned, following Val at top speed to the kitchen.

"Oh, boy, Erin, are you ever dumb!" Teddy said, as he and Erin trotted after Val and Doc.

"Well, I kind of forgot about the laundry room," Erin admitted weakly.

All four Taylors clattered down the basement stairs. Val reached the laundry first, took one look, and wailed, "Not again! It's the third snowstorm in one week!"

Sure enough, the floor was covered with white soap powder. The little monkey was sitting in a basket full of clean clothes, trying to figure out how to put on one of Erin's leotards. She'd pulled a sock of Teddy's over her head so it looked as though she was wearing a stocking cap. Other clothes were scattered across the floor, liberally sprinkled with soap. The smell of chlorine stung Val's eyes and nose, and she saw that the bleach bottle was lying on its side, the cap off, on top of Doc's favorite pair of jeans. The jeans were no longer solid blue — there was a big white splotch down one leg.

Gigi began to chatter cheerfully, but broke off as Val lunged for her. Still wearing the sock on her head, she jumped on top of the washer, not realizing that the lid was open, and fell right inside.

"Gotcha!" Val yelled. She was sorely tempted to slam the lid down and leave Gigi in there, but she resisted and merely scooped the little monkey up. Gigi covered her face with her hands, burying her head in Val's shoulder.

"I know," Erin said sadly. "I have to clean up the mess. Again."

"We'll help," Doc told her. "Vallie, take that little beast upstairs, batten down the hatches in your room, and shut her in. Teddy, lend a hand." He picked up his sodden, bleached-out jeans. "My favorite jeans . . ." he said with a sigh.

"Hey, Dad, I have a great idea," Teddy said as he started picking up the clothing from the floor. "How about we take Gigi to Wildlife Farm tomorrow instead of Sunday — or maybe even tonight!"

"That *is* a great idea," Erin added. "How about right this minute?"

"I wouldn't mind," Doc said, "but Wildlife Farm doesn't open until ten o'clock tomorrow morning and Animal Inn opens at nine, so I'm afraid we'll have to wait until Sunday."

"Well, Gigi, you seem to have lost your champions," Val told the monkey as she carried Gigi upstairs. "Believe me, you're just going to *love* it at Wildlife Farm — and we're going to love it when you're gone."

On Sunday afternoon shortly after two o'clock, Animal Inn's vet van was cruising along the highway on the way to Wildlife Farm. Val and Erin sat up front with Doc. Erin was holding Gigi on her lap. The little monkey was wearing a ruffled dress that had once belonged to Erin's doll, Elizabeth. She looked, Val thought, like a skinny, ugly child. But her fur was shiny, and her eyes shone, too, with excitement and mischief. It was hard to believe that this was the same animal that the Taylors had rescued from Zefferelli's Kosmic Karnival such a short time ago. That Gigi had been dirty, scruffy, runny-nosed, undernourished, and barely strong enough to raise her head. This Gigi was ready to take on the world — and the world had better watch out. Did Wildlife Farm have any idea what a little bundle of energy they were about to receive? Val very much doubted it.

"How much longer, Dad?" Teddy asked, leaning over the seat. He and Toby were in the rear of the van with Little Leo. The lion cub was draped across Toby's lap, his big, fat paws resting on the seat. Little Leo, too, was a far cry from the scrawny, filthy creature he'd been when Val had first laid eyes on him. He had had his long-awaited bath, and though he was far from being fat, he was definitely filling out. It wouldn't be long before he'd look like the young prince he really was.

"About ten minutes, I think," Doc said. "There's supposed to be a sign coming up on the right. Keep your eyes peeled."

Val reached over the seat and scratched Little Leo's head.

"I know it's not possible, but he looks like he's grown another foot," she said.

Toby shook his head and said with a straight face, "You're right. It's not possible. He still only has four."

Val stuck her tongue out at him. "Very funny!"

"I see it — the sign for Wildlife Farm," Erin cried. "Right over there. See?"

Doc slowed the van and signaled for the turn, then turned off the highway onto a narrow road. Now there were signs everywhere: WILDLIFE FARM — ONE MILE; WILDLIFE FARM — ONE-HALF MILE; WILDLIFE FARM — FIFTY FEET.

"We're here!" Teddy crowed as Doc drove the

van under a big wooden sign that spanned an even narrower road. WELCOME TO WILDLIFE FARM, the sign said.

Val, Erin, Teddy, and Toby craned their necks, looking from side to side. It was like a vast park, with fenced areas where all sorts of animals roamed.

"Look! Buffaloes!" Teddy shouted.

"And deer. Aren't they graceful and pretty?" cried Erin.

"Hey — isn't that a zebra?" Toby asked.

"Nope — it's a horse in striped pajamas," Teddy joked.

"I see some bears over there," Val said. "Nice, healthy-looking ones, too."

Doc drove very slowly down the road and finally stopped in a parking lot in front of what looked like an administration building. It was a long, low log structure with beds of bright chrysanthemums on either side of the main entrance.

"You wait here," Doc said. "I'll go in and find out where we should take Gigi and Little Leo."

Gigi struggled to escape Erin's grasp and follow Doc, but she and Val hung onto the little monkey.

"In a minute, Gigi," Val said. "I'm glad you're so eager to check out your new home."

"Oh, dear," Erin sighed. "Now that we're here, I'm not sure this was a good idea. I'm going to miss Gigi. She looks so adorable in that little dress."

"Yes, and she looked adorable swinging from the curtain rod after she tore up my essay," Val said. "Not to mention covered with flour in the pantry, and up to her knees in soap powder!"

"I guess you're right," Erin admitted. "But I'm going to miss her, anyway."

"Me, too," Teddy said. "And I'll miss good ol' Leo here."

"Little Leo's my pal, aren't you, fella?" Toby said gruffly, stroking the lion cub's head. "I even asked my dad if we could maybe keep him on the farm, but he said no way. Cows and lions don't mix, he said, and I guess he's right."

"I thought Mrs. Racer was going to cry when we told her Sunday would be Gigi's last day with us," Erin said.

"They might have been tears of relief," Val told her. "She knows it's for the best. The next time we come back to visit, she's going to come, too."

"Here comes Dad," Teddy said.

Doc got back into the van and started the engine. "We're supposed to go around behind this building and down a dirt road to the left," he said. "The monkey house is right next to the lion's den, so Gigi and Leo will be able to keep in touch." Then he grinned. "And Gigi has a surprise in store for her, I understand."

"A surprise? What kind of surprise?" Erin asked.

"If I told you, it wouldn't be a surprise anymore, would it?"

"Oh, Daddy, you *always* say that!" Erin pouted.

"That's because it's true," Doc said.

Barely a minute later, he stopped the van in front of two large fenced enclosures. Both were roofed and walled with sturdy wire netting, and both had several large trees inside. From a tree in the smaller enclosure hung a tire on a rope, and a little trapeze.

A teenage girl in jeans and a T-shirt that said WILDLIFE FARM across the front came to meet them as Val, Teddy, Erin and Gigi, and Toby and Little Leo piled out of the van after Doc.

"Hi. I'm Melissa. This is where Gigi and Little Leo are going to live," she said, smiling and revealing a mouthful of braces. "We're so excited! We've been wanting a lion, and they're not easy to come by."

She knelt down beside Little Leo and rubbed behind his ears. "You're going to be a beauty when you grow up," she told him. "As a matter of fact, you're not so bad right now."

Little Leo rumbled and looked pleased. The girl opened the gate of the larger enclosure and motioned for Toby to bring Little Leo in. She turned to Erin.

"I love the monkey's dress!" she said. "But maybe you better take it off before you let her go. It might get tangled up in the branches of the trees."

Sadly, Erin removed the little ruffled dress. "I

hope she's not going to be too lonely," she said. "She's used to having lots of people around."

"Oh, there are plenty of people here all the time," Melissa assured her. "But even in the wintertime, I guarantee she won't be lonely. She and Little Leo will have warm houses to live in when it gets cold — and Gigi will have Elmer to play with."

"Elmer? Who's Elmer?" Val asked.

Melissa walked over to the tallest tree and gave a piercing whistle. The branches quivered, and suddenly another capuchin monkey appeared, skittering down the tree trunk. Gigi took one look and leaped out of Erin's arms, chattering loudly. Elmer chattered back. Moments later, Gigi and Elmer were swinging through the trees side-by-side.

"That was the surprise," Doc told Erin. "Elmer just arrived yesterday."

"Oh," Erin said in a small voice.

"Aren't you glad that Gigi's found a friend?" Val asked.

"I guess," Erin said. "But I kind of wish she'd said good-bye or something." She looked down at the doll dress in her hand. "I guess she didn't really care about us after all."

"Sure she did, honey," Doc said, putting his arm around her. "But she's all excited at finding another monkey to play with. Think how you'd feel if you'd been living with a family of monkeys and all of a sudden you met a child your own age. You'd be excited, too."

"I suppose so," Erin said.

Melissa led the way out of the monkeys' enclosure and fastened the gate securely. Val joined Toby and Teddy next door, where Little Leo was investigating his new home. He'd found a big hard rubber ball, and was batting it around like an overgrown kitten.

"Oh, Mommy, look at the baby lion!" a child cried, dragging his mother over to watch. Several other people came over, too, and soon there was an admiring, laughing crowd enjoying the antics of Little Leo, Gigi, and Elmer.

Val gave Little Leo a farewell pat. Then she, Toby, and Teddy came outside and Melissa fastened that gate, too.

"See you next week, Leo," Teddy called. "You, too, Gigi." He turned to his father. "Hey, Dad, can we go look at the other animals now? I want to see a real buffalo up close."

"Sure thing," Doc said. He took Teddy's and Erin's hands. "I think I saw a sign advertising pony rides, too. That sound like fun?"

Erin brightened a little. "Yes, I'd like that." She looked over her shoulder. " 'Bye, Gigi. Have fun with your new friend," she said, going off with Doc and Teddy in search of ponies and buffalo.

Val and Toby lingered behind.

"You know," Val said, "I've been thinking. I've been blaming Gigi for the whole mess over my essay, and in a way it *was* her fault. But on the other hand, if she hadn't torn up my first copy, I wouldn't have had to type it again, and if I hadn't typed it again, I probably wouldn't have remembered every single word, and Lila would have won the contest after all."

"So what you're saying is, you owe your prize to Gigi, right?" Toby asked.

"Right," Val agreed. "Hey, look! Here she comes."

Gigi swung down from the little trapeze and loped over the ground to where Val and Toby were standing. She scrambled up the wire netting, and stretched out one skinny arm.

Grinning, Val took the little paw and shook it. "Thanks, partner," she said.

Gigi grinned, too, clinging to Val's fingers. Then with a squawk and a stream of happy chatter, she ran back to the tree where Elmer was waiting. Val grabbed Toby's hand.

"Come on! Let's catch up to Dad and the others," she said. "I'll race you!"

Laughing, Val and Toby sprinted off.